JACKSON GRISHAM

# The Unstoppable Evil

*To my family, who taught me the meaning of courage and resilience.*
*To the dreamers, the wanderers, and the believers who dare to hope.*
*And to the heroes we never see but whose sacrifices shape the world—*
*This book is for you.*

"Not all those who wander are lost."
—J.R.R. Tolkien

# Contents

# Foreword

When I began crafting this story, I was struck by the timeless allure of courage in the face of insurmountable odds. Much like the myths and legends that have guided humanity through the ages, this tale is born from a desire to explore the resilience of the human spirit and the lengths we go to for hope, unity, and survival.

Inspired by epic journeys like Tolkien's *The Lord of the Rings*, this novel seeks to delve into the struggle between light and darkness, not only in the world around us but also within ourselves. It is a story of camaraderie, sacrifice, and the enduring power of love and loyalty.

As you turn the pages, my hope is that you find echoes of the struggles we face in our own lives, and that through the bravery of these characters, you are reminded of the light we all carry, no matter how dark the world may seem.

Thank you for embarking on this journey with me.

—Jackson Grisham

# Preface

Stories have always had the power to shape and inspire, to remind us of who we are and who we strive to be. This novel was born from a deep admiration for the epic sagas that have stood the test of time. Yet, it is also uniquely its own—a story shaped by modern challenges, timeless truths, and the enduring fight for unity in the face of division.

When I first imagined the world of Elarion, it was as a vast canvas painted with both despair and hope. This is a tale of flawed heroes and unexpected alliances, where the smallest acts of courage can have the greatest impact.

As the author, I feel immensely privileged to share this story with you. It is my hope that you find adventure in its pages, strength in its characters, and inspiration in their trials. May it remind us all that even in our darkest hours, we possess the power to light the way.

—Jackson Grisham

# Acknowledgments

No novel is written in isolation, and this one is no exception. I owe a debt of gratitude to many who made this book possible:

To my editor, whose keen eye and unrelenting passion shaped this story into its final form—thank you for believing in the vision.

To my friends and beta readers, who weathered countless drafts and offered invaluable feedback, your insights were a guiding light.

To my family, whose unwavering support and patience allowed me the time and space to create—thank you for standing by me through it all.

To the authors and storytellers who inspired me—Tolkien, Lewis, Le Guin, and others—you've shown me the magic of creating entire worlds.

And finally, to you, the reader—thank you for picking up this book and stepping into the world I've created. This journey belongs to you now.

With gratitude,

Jackson Grisham

# 1

# The Ancient Prophecy

The early morning light broke over the village of **Rivenmere**, painting its thatched roofs and cobblestone streets in hues of gold and amber. Birds chirped their songs; the melody carried on a cool breeze that whispered through the surrounding forests. It was a serene scene that seemed the world beyond did not exist—no wars, kings, or distant empires. For the villagers, the day promised nothing more than the simplicity of routine as they tended to crops, livestock, and the occasional festival preparations.

For Kael, this day started like any other: with a sharp nudge courtesy of his little sister, Mina.

"Kael! You lazy mule, get up!" Mina's voice cut through the soft warmth of sleep. "The morning market won't set up itself!"

Kael groaned, rolling over on the straw mattress of their small home. At nineteen, he was tall and wiry, with unruly brown hair that seemed determined to defy every attempt to restrain it. Two years his junior, Mina was his complete opposite—sharp-tongued and bouncing with energy, with an uncanny ability to command the attention of anyone within earshot.

"I'm up," he muttered, though he wasn't.

"You're hopeless," Mina sighed, yanking the blanket off him.

Kael stretched, reluctantly sitting up and rubbing his eyes. Outside, the village gradually stirred: pots clanged, cattle lowed, and neighbors' murmurs reached distant and indistinct. The air smelled of dew and newly baked bread.

It should have been another peaceful day in Rivenmere, but something subtle yet undeniable unease hung in the air. Kael felt this even before the events of that morning unfolded.

The Stranger Arrives

The first sign of change came mid-morning, as Kael helped Mina arrange baskets of herbs and roots at their stall in the market square. As usual, the square was teeming to capacity, with villagers haggling over goods and swapping rumors. Kael's mind wandered as he worked, a life beyond Rivenmere's borders dancing in his mind.

It was then that the stranger appeared.

He was tall and cloaked, his dark robes tattered and dusted with the dirt of a long journey. A staff carved with intricate runes tapped against the cobblestones at every step he took. A hood shrouded his face, though now and then, Kael saw flashes of sharp features and eyes that seemed to pierce through the mundane scene before him.

The villagers did, too, their conversations faltering as he passed. Strangers were rare in Rivenmere, a village in the farthest corner of the Kingdom of Velorn. Travelers avoided the place, claiming it was too remote to bother with.

Kael shivered as the stranger's gaze swept over the market, pausing briefly on him.

"Who is that?" Mina whispered, clenching Kael's arm.

"I don't know," Kael replied, equally transfixed.

The stranger halted in the middle of the square, in the eye of every onlooker. As he spoke, his tone had a timbre that brooked attention.

"I seek the one called Kael," he declared, his words cutting through the silent air.

Kael's heart pounded as he froze. How did this man know his name?

The villagers were turning to him, their murmurs of confusion alive on their faces. Mina's grip on his arm tightened.

"Don't answer," she hissed.

But the stranger's gaze was locked on him, unyielding. Kael stepped forward, swallowing the lump in his throat.

"I'm Kael," he said, his voice steadier than he felt. "Who's asking?"

The stranger lowered his hood, revealing a face weathered by time and burden. His silver hair was tied back, and his eyes glimmered with the knowledge of one who had seen centuries pass.

"I am Eryndor, Keeper of the Arcane Lore," he said. "And you, Kael of Rivenmere, are destined to save this world."

The square erupted into whispers and exclamations. Kael felt the weight of every eye on him. He opened his mouth to protest, but Eryndor raised a hand, silencing the crowd.

"Your questions will be answered," the mage said, his voice brooking no defiance. "But not here. The shadows have ears, and time is short."

Eryndor motioned for Kael to follow, striding toward the edge of the village. Mina grabbed Kael's arm.

"You can't just go with him!" she said.

Kael hesitated. Every instinct screamed at him to stay, to refuse this absurd claim. And yet, something more profound—an inexplicable pull—urged him forward.

"I'll be back," he told Mina, though he wasn't sure he believed it.

Reluctantly, he followed Eryndor out of the square, past the fields, and into the dense forest beyond.

They walked in silence for what seemed to be hours, the treetops of the forest canopy above casting shimmering patterns of light and shade on the ground. Finally, Eryndor stopped in a small clearing, where a felled log served as a bench. He motioned for Kael to sit.

"Why me?" Kael asked, breaking the silence.

Eryndor leaned on his staff, his expression grave. "Because the prophecy speaks of you. 'The one born under the shadow of the crescent moon, who carries the blood of the first king, shall rise against the darkness.' That is you, Kael."

Kael shook his head. "There must be some mistake. I'm just a farmer's son. I've never even left Rivenmere."

"The prophecy does not make mistakes," Eryndor said firmly. "In your veins flows the bloodline of the first king, even if that is unknown to you. The darkness grows once more, much as it did in the age of the Crown of Shadows."

At the mention of the Crown, a shiver ran down Kael's spine. Everyone in Velorn knew the stories of how the Crown had given its wearer great power but at the cost of his humanity and that the last to wield it had plunged the world into centuries of war and suffering.

"I thought the Crown was destroyed," Kael said.

"So we thought," Eryndor said. "Yet it had not been destroyed- only well concealed. And now, by its heir, it is sought to be regained. If he can succeed, the world as we know it will fall into the darkness of eternity."

Kael stared hard at the mage to comprehend the enormity of the tale he was listening to. "And you think I can stop this? How?

Eryndor reached deep within his robes and pulled out a small, glowing crystal. Its warm yet otherworldly light pulsed faintly in his hand.

"This is the Shard of Illumina," he said. "One of the few relics capable of countering the Crown's power. But it is incomplete. To destroy the Crown, we must find the other shards scattered across the realms and guarded by trials and dangers beyond imagining."

Kael's mind reeled. This was madness. He was no warrior, no hero from the old tales. He was just a boy from Rivenmere.

"I can't do this," he said, rising suddenly. "You've got the wrong person."

Eryndor's eyes seemed to bore into his very soul. "You can, Kael. And you must. The darkness will not wait. Already, its minions are on the move. If you do nothing, they will come for you, your family, your village. There is no escaping this."

The First Attack

A chilling howl echoed through the forest as if to punctuate Eryndor's words. Kael froze, his heart pounding.

"They've found us," Eryndor said grimly, gripping his staff.

Before Kael could ask what he meant, the trees around them seemed to shift and darken. Shadows, great hulking, twisted creatures with glowing red eyes coalesced into shapes.

"Shadowbeasts," Eryndor explained. "Stay behind me."

The beasts charged, their talons mirroring obsidian. Eryndor hefted his staff, and a burst of light erupted from the crystal, forcing them to retreat.

Kael fell and scrambled to his feet as his instincts screamed to flee. But something inside Kael snapped- a surge of bravery he did not know he possessed. Picking up a fallen branch, he swung at one of the creatures in a wide arc, which had just enough shock value for Eryndor to end with a burst of magic.

The fight was over instantly, but the message remained clear: the darkness would not stop.

Eryndor turned to him, his face deadly serious. "This is only the beginning. Should you not act, many more will come for you and for everyone you love."

Kael looked down at the fallen creatures, back to Eryndor. The weight of the choice facing him seemed to sink in for the first time.

"I'll go with you," he said quietly. "But if this prophecy is wrong, you'll regret dragging me into it."

Eryndor's lips curved into a faint smile. "The prophecy is never wrong. Come,

Kael. Our journey begins now."

The quiet forest seemed to hold its breath as Kael and Eryndor stood amidst the shadows of the slain beasts. The air was thick with the metallic scent of battle and the faint hum of residual magic. Kael's hands were still shaking, and the broken branch he had used to fend off one of the creatures was tightly in his grasp.

Eryndor turned to him then, his piercing eyes softer now, though still shadowed by the burden he carried.

"You fought well for someone untrained," the mage said, voice measured yet carrying a note of approval.

Kael shook his head, throwing the branch to the ground. "I didn't fight. I panicked."

"Fear is natural," Eryndor said, leaning on his staff. "But you stood your ground. That is more than most would do."

Kael didn't respond. His mind was in turmoil of emotions in a whirlwind fashion: fear, disbelief, anger, and a strange certainty. He turned to the twisted forms of the shadow beasts, now dissolving into dark mist. What kind of world had he just been pulled into?

The trip back to the village was apprehensive. Kael was keenly aware of every rustling leaf and snapping twig, half-expecting another ambush. Eryndor strode ahead; his staff tapped a steady rhythm against the forest floor.

As they reached the outskirts of Rivenmere, Kael abruptly stopped.

"I need to tell Mina," he said, his voice firm.

Eryndor turned, his expression unreadable. "You cannot delay. The longer we linger, the greater the danger to this village."

"Then she deserves to know why I'm leaving," Kael said. "I can't just disappear without a word."

Eryndor studied him for a long moment before nodding. "Very well. But be quick. The shadows do not rest."

Kael hurried back to his house, where his heart pounded. Mina was inside, nervously pacing near the fireplace. Upon seeing him, her face brightened with relief, quickly clouding again as she glanced at his jaw set.

"What happened? Who is that man?" she pressed insistently.

Kael hesitated, not quite sure how to explain the enormity of what had just transpired. He settled for the truth as best as he could manage.

"Mina, I have to go. There's. Something is coming-something larger than us. That man, Eryndor, says I'm part of it."

Mina's eyes flashed wide. "Leave? Are you insane? What could be so important that you'd abandon everything?"

Kael put a hand on her shoulder, attempting to still his nervousness as much as hers. "I don't understand it all yet. But those creatures in the woods-they were real, Mina. And they'll come here if I don't go."

Tears welled in her eyes, but she bit her lip and nodded. "Then go. But promise me you'll come back. Promise me this isn't goodbye."

Kael pulled her into a hug, his throat tightening. "I promise."

Into the Unknown

Kael met Eryndor at the village gates, a small pouch slung over his shoulder. It contained little more than a spare tunic, some bread, and a waterskin. The mage gave him a curt nod and turned to lead the way.

As they left Rivenmere behind, a pang of guilt twisted within Kael's gut. For nineteen years, the village had been his whole world; now he was leaving it, maybe forever.

The road ahead was a long sweep, winding through forests and rolling hills. Eryndor set a rapid pace, saying little. As they walked, Kael's thoughts churned, swarming with questions he didn't know how to ask. Finally, he broke the silence.

"You said the prophecy speaks of me," he began, his tone sheepish. "But how do you know it's true? What if you've made a mistake?"

Eryndor looked at him once, inscrutable. "Prophecies are not always clear, yet the signs do not deceive. You were born under the crescent moon, as it was told. And the blood of the first king runs in your veins, though you may not know that yet."

Kael frowned. "What does that even mean? My parents were farmers, not royalty."

"There is much about your lineage hidden from you," Eryndor said. "In time, you will learn the truth. But for now, trust that your role is not a coincidence."

Kael was silent then, his mind racing. Was it possible? Could he be the descendant of kings? It couldn't be, and neither could most of what had happened that day.

The First Night on the Road

When the sun began to set below the horizon, Kael's legs hurt, and his stomach protested loudly. They stopped by a small stream, where Eryndor gathered wood for a fire.

As the fire crackled to life, Kael sat cross-legged, tearing into a piece of bread from his pouch. Eryndor, however, seemed content to sit in silence, staring into the fire as if lost in thought.

Kael couldn't stand the quiet any longer. "You've done this before, haven't you? Found someone because of a prophecy, I mean."

Eryndor's eyes didn't leave the fire. "I have guided others, yes. But your path is singular."

"What of them?" Kael asked insistently.

Eryndor tucked a moment, and Kael saw a flicker of something—pain, perhaps—in the old mage's eyes for the first time.

"Some succeeded," he replied low. "Others. did not."

Kael's appetite was gone. He stared into the fire, the weight of Eryndor's words settling heavily on his shoulders.

A Taste of Power

Eryndor pulled the Shard of Illumina from his robes as the fire burned low. The crystal's light bathed the clearing in soft, ethereal radiance and cast long shadows against the trees.

Kael leaned forward, mesmerized. "What is that, exactly? You called it a shard."

"It is a fragment of the original Illumina Stone," Eryndor said. "A relic of immense power, forged in the age of the first kings. It is one of the few forces capable of countering the Crown of Shadows."

Kael reached out instinctively, but Eryndor drew the shard back.

"It is not a trinket," the mage said sharply. "Its power is not to be taken lightly."

Kael pulled his hand back and chided. "Why show it to me, then?"

"Because you must understand what is at stake," Eryndor said. "This shard is both a weapon and a key. But it is incomplete. To fulfill its purpose, we must find the others."

"And where are they?" Kael asked.

Eryndor sighed. "Scattered across the realms, hidden in places of great peril. Ancient wards and powerful foes guard each. Retrieving them will test us in ways you cannot yet imagine."

Kael felt a chill despite the warmth of the fire. He had barely survived one fight against shadow beasts. How could he possibly face the dangers Eryndor described?

The Night Watch

Eryndor insisted on taking the first watch when the fire burned down. Kael settled down on the hard, unforgiving earth, his suitcase as a pillow. He didn't find sleep coming quickly.

He stared at the canopy of stars above, his mind a jumbled mess of fear and doubt. What had he gotten himself into? He wasn't a hero. He wasn't even brave. He was just Kael, a boy from Rivenmere.

Yet, profound inside, a fire of determination started to grow. He didn't understand the prophecy and didn't believe he was the savior Eryndor claimed him to be. But he could not disregard one thing: the shadowbeasts were real, and the danger they posed wasn't going anywhere.

If he didn't act, who would?

As sleep finally claimed him, Kael's dreams were filled with the vision of some far-off lands and fierce battles for a crown wreathed in darkness.

# 2

# Call of the Kingdom

The morning sun broke through the treetops, casting dappled light onto the path ahead. The soft chirping of birds and the distant rush of a waterfall were the only sounds that accompanied Kael as he followed Eryndor through the forest. The air felt fresher than it had in years, and despite the previous day's events, Kael couldn't help but feel a sense of strange calm.

They had been riding since morning, but the steep wilderness kept them at a moderate pace. Kael's legs ached, yet his mind swirled with all the questions brewing since leaving Rivenmere. Eryndor had remained silent all morning, speaking only as he had to, at an unhurried, even pace. Kael labored to keep up with him, older by a generation and continued to push himself onward, determined to glean more about the dangerous mission that was now his reality.

They stopped to rest briefly under the canopy of tall oak trees whose leaves danced gently in the breeze. Kael sat on soft grass, working his fingers through his hair as he tried to clear his mind. Eryndor was relaxed and cross-legged, and his staff lay beside him on the ground.

"Master Eryndor," Kael began, breaking the silence. His voice came out smaller than he had meant, but he forced the words out. "You spoke of the Crown of

Shadows. What is that exactly? And why is it so dangerous?

The shadows deepened in Eryndor's eyes, and he looked away into the distance. It seemed to Kael for a moment that the mage would dodge the question, as he had dodged so many others, but then he spoke in a manner as calculated and filled with an unmistakable weight.

"The Crown of Shadows is more ancient than the kingdoms themselves. The dark sorcerers who, until long ago, ruled over these lands created it before even the first kings and queens ascended to power. It symbolizes control, taming the forces of darkness that would devour our world. They say whoever wears the crown can bend the shadows to his will, unleashing destruction and chaos upon all living things."

Kael listened closely, his heart heavy from Eryndor's words. He had never heard of such a thing before, but a sense of dread crept into his chest as the mage continued.

"But the crown is not only dangerous because it can control the shadows," Eryndor continued. "It is also accursed. Those who wear it are bound to it, losing their humanity bit by bit until they become no more than vessels for the darkness itself. The last time the crown was worn, it nearly tore the world. The kingdoms were thrown into war, and many lives were lost. It was only through the effort of the first king that the crown was sealed away, hidden from the eyes of men."

Kael frowned, trying to make sense of it all. "And now the crown has resurfaced?"

Eryndor nodded, his eyes narrowing with a shade of worry. "Yes. The shadows have started to stir once more, and the crown is becoming increasingly powerful. It will only be a question of time before the location of the crown is discovered and somebody attempts to take it. That is why you need to find the shards of Illumina. Only with those shards can we hope to prevent the crown from falling into the wrong hands."

The words of the mage ran a shiver down Kael's spine. The thought that a crown could do such a thing was almost inconceivable. Yet, impossible as it seemed, it was becoming increasingly obvious that this was indeed the threat he was being set to thwart. But where was he to find these shards? And what part did he–a mere farmer's son–play in it all?

"You said the shards are hidden across the realms," Kael said slowly, his tone uncertain. "But how are we to find them? What if they are lost forever?

"We shall seek them out," Eryndor said matter-of-factly. "It won't be easy, and it will take time. But we will not be left to the task alone. There are others, too, who seek, others who share a common purpose. And we must find them before the minions of darkness do."

Kael looked up at the mage, his eyes wide in confusion. "Others? Whom?

Eryndor hesitated, his gaze flashing to the horizon before returning to Kael. "There are many who have been chosen by fate, just as you have. Some of them do not even know their destiny, while others have known for far longer. But we must seek them out, because these will be those allies that shall prove crucial to our success."

Kael nodded, doing his best to take it all in. It was a lot to swallow, and he wasn't so sure he was ready for the weight of this responsibility. But one thing was for sure–he couldn't turn his back upon it now. Whatever lay ahead in the form of dangers, he would face it. For Rivenmere, for Mina, and for the future of the world.

The Hidden Village

The sun beat higher into the sky; Eryndor and Kael pressed on, deeper into the forest. Hours passed in near silence, an odd word exchanged now and then. Heavier as their conversation was getting, Kael found he was starting to fall into the rhythm of the road. His body was growing used to the exertion, while his mind was focusing on the tasks at hand.

As they approached the small clearing, Kael's stomach was rumbling, and he knew Eryndor was beginning to feel the same strain of their long journey. They had travelled for nearly half a day, and it was time for another rest. He nodded at a little hut nestled among the trees-a small shack-like affair that, to most, was out of place in the heart of the wilderness.

"This is where we will spend the night," Eryndor said, guiding Kael toward the hut. "It is a safe house, known only to a few."

Kael followed him inside, his eyes scanning the modest interior. The hut was small, yet cozy, and there was a low wooden table with several chairs here and there. A fire smoldered in the hearth, filling the air with warmth and the scent of burning wood. There were shelves full of herbs and scrolls, and in one corner, Kael noticed a stack of maps.

"You have been here before," Kael said, curiously. "Who else knows of this place?"

Eryndor was silent for a moment; his fingers touched the edges of a map. "There are those who protect the secrets of the realms, those whose life's work has gone toward maintaining the balance. This place is one of many, tucked away across the lands-safe havens for those who know what is to come."

Kael sat down in the chair, his mind reeling with an attempt to digest it all. Safe havens? Realms? Balance? It was all so out of this world. Yet, the shadowbeasts, the Crown of Shadows-it was irrevocably clear that the world was a great deal larger and more complicating than he had ever fathomed.

"I'm starting to understand," Kael said slowly, his voice uncertain. "But I still don't know how I fit into all of this. I'm just a farmer, Eryndor. What could I possibly do to stop something like the Crown of Shadows?"

Eryndor took a seat across from him, and quiet wisdom bathed his eyes. "You are not just a farmer, Kael. You are the heir to a legacy reaching back through the ages. The blood of the first king courses through your veins, and with it comes a power you have yet to find. You are more capable than you realize.

Kael opened his mouth to protest, but a raised hand from Eryndor silenced him.

"I know you doubt yourself," the mage continued. "But there is no turning back. The shadows will not wait for you to be ready. The world is changing, and you must change with it."

The Revelation

When night fell and the fire crackled in the hearth, Eryndor pulled out a worn leather-bound tome from his bag. He laid it on the table before Kael, and for the first time, Kael saw the true weight of what was at stake.

"This," Eryndor said in his low voice, "is the Book of Shadows. It contains the knowledge of the ancient sorcerers-the ones that created the Crown of Shadows. It also contains the prophecy that speaks of the shards of Illumina."

Kael's fingers hovered over the book, feeling a strange pull as if the very pages contained the answers he had been seeking. Eryndor opened it with caution and revealed an intricate map of the realms-a map that pulsed with a faint light.

"This is where our journey begins," Eryndor said softly. "The map shows the locations of the shards. But there are trials we must face to reach them. Trials that will test everything we know about ourselves."

Kael nodded, steeling himself for the challenges ahead. The path he had chosen was dangerous, but it was the only one that could save Rivenmere—and perhaps the world.

The morning after their arrival at the secluded hut, Kael woke to the sound of birds singing outside. He felt the weight of the mission pressing on him, but the strange calm from yesterday still lingered. Eryndor had remained silent about the specifics of their next steps, but Kael could sense that something important was about to unfold. After a quick breakfast of dried meats and berries, they packed their things and set off once again, this time with renewed purpose.

The forest around them was thick with its tall trees almost seeming to shut in as they moved deeper into the wilds. The air was thick with pine scent and earth, and the far hum of insects filled stillness. As they went, Kael couldn't avoid the question of what mysterious shards Eryndor had talked about. Where were they hidden? How could they be found? And most of all, why was Kael to be saddled with an impossible task such as this?

"We have to get to the Eldergrove," Eryndor's voice cut into Kael's musing. "It's where the first shard lies."

Kael turned to him, his brow furrowed in question. "The Eldergrove? Where's that?"

Eryndor's gaze slid forward, his eyes unreadable. "It is a place of great power. A sacred site, far in from the forest depths. The trees there are more ancient than any other in this realm. It is said that the first shard of Illumina resides deep in the heart of Eldergrove, watched over by a protector who has stood duty for centuries."

"A creature?" Kael repeated, as unease seeped into his voice. "What kind of creature?"

Eryndor's lips curled into a weak, mirthless smile. "A guardian, Kael. It is neither friend nor foe, but it will not let us take the shard without proving ourselves worthy."

Kael fell silent, his eyes reflecting on the gravity of the situation. A creature? A guardian? It was far different from life in Rivenmere, yet here he was, so far away from home and walking toward a mysterious forest to face an unknown guardian. If he was honest with himself, he was terrified. More than anything else, he felt a deep sense of responsibility. Rivenmere was counting on him, and the fate of the realm rested in his hands.

They walked in silence for what felt like hours, the only sound coming from leaves crunching beneath their feet to break the stillness. The farther they traveled, the thicker the woods grew, and the air thickened with the scent of moss and ancient trees. The path eventually narrowed ahead, and the group was forced into single file. Eryndor's face was set, his eyes scouring the surroundings as one who had done so many times before. Yet Kael could not rid himself of the feeling they were being watched.

Just as he was about to speak, Eryndor held up a hand, signaling them to stop. The mage's eyes were narrowed, his senses alert. Kael followed his gaze, but all he could see were the trees stretching into the distance, their twisted branches reaching for the sky.

"The Eldergrove is close," Eryndor said softly, his voice barely above a whisper. "We must be cautious now."

They kept moving forward, their steps more deliberate. It felt almost as if the forest itself was changing around them, growing more alive and more aware. The trees grew taller, widening, their bark thick with age. It was as if the very earth beneath their feet coursed with energy. Kael's heartbeat quickened in response, and he found himself holding his breath, waiting for something, anything, to happen.

They burst into a clearing.

Before them opened the Eldergrove, ancient trees so wide it would take many strides to circumnavigate their trunks, living monuments. The air was thick with magic here, and Kael could feel it swirling around him, pressing against his skin like a physical force. In the very center of that grove was a great stone altar, overgrown with vines and moss, its surface etched with runes of old that glowed faintly in the dimness. The treetops seemed to lean in over it, as if watching it, guarding it.

"This is it," Eryndor said in a hushed tone, his voice filled with wonder. "The first shard is here, hidden within the altar. But we shall have to be careful. The guardian will test us."

Before Kael could ask what the test would be, a low rumbling sound shook the grove. The ground beneath their feet began to quake, and the air grew still, as if the world itself was holding its breath. From the shadows of the trees, a figure began to emerge.

Kael's heart leaped into his throat as the creature stepped into the clearing. It was unlike anything he had ever seen. It stood at least ten feet tall, its body composed of twisting tendrils of energy that shifted and writhed in the air. Its face was a mask of glowing runes, its eyes burning with some otherworldly fire. Moving with grace, its mere existence overwhelmed him, as if carrying the weight of centuries upon its shoulders.

Before them stood the guardian, his eyes fixed upon Kael, and for one moment the air was heavy with a hushed, tense silence. Eryndor stepped forward, raising his staff in a sign of respect, but the creature made no show of recognizing him. Its attention belonged solely to Kael.

"You seek the shard of Illumina," said the guardian, his words like a thousand whispers, each heavy with an ancientness of power. "But what makes you worthy of it? What will you sacrifice to claim it?"

Kael swallowed hard, his mind racing. Sacrifice? He had no idea what this creature was asking, but he knew one thing: the shard had to be obtained. For Rivenmere. For the world. But at what price?

"I—" Kael started, but his voice broke down under the weight of the guardian's stare. He could feel its power bearing down upon him, testing his resolve. "I don't know what you want from me," he said finally, his voice barely above a whisper. "But I will do whatever it takes to protect my people. To stop the darkness from consuming everything."

The guardian's eyes flared brighter, and for a moment Kael thought it might attack. But instead the creature stepped aside, its form shifting and re-forming in the air as it circled around him. The whispers grew louder, more insistent, filling his mind with images of his past-his quiet life in Rivenmere, his family, the friends he had lost. The people who depended on him.

"To claim the shard," the guardian intoned, "you must prove your heart. You must face your deepest fear and emerge stronger than before."

Kael's stomach churned. His deepest fear? What could that possibly be? He had lost so much already-was there anything left to fear?

The guardian began to blink out of form, shudder and distort, until suddenly Kael was otherwhere. He was not in the Eldergrove anymore. He was back in Rivenmere. There the familiar market square was before him, with the modest dwellings and the far hills behind. Yet everything was wrong.

The village was ablaze, smoke curled in every direction into the sky. People ran wildly through the streets, faces contorted in fear and pain. The air was thick with the cacophony of screams and clashing steel. Kael's heart raced as he searched for someone-anyone-among the chaos.

And then, he saw her.

Mina.

She stood in the middle of the street, her eyes on Kael. But something was off about her. She was not the girl he remembered. Her face was pale, her eyes wide with terror. Then, before Kael's very eyes, she started to crumble, her body disintegrating into dust and releasing itself to the air.

Kael screamed, running forward, but he was already too late. Mina was gone.

The vision burst apart, and Kael stood in the Eldergrove once more, gasping for air. The guardian stood before him, its eyes pitiless.

"You have faced your fear," it said, its voice soft now. "But have you learned from it?"

Kael swallowed, his hands shaking. "I-I don't know if I can do this," he whispered, his voice cracking. "I don't know if I'm strong enough."

"You are," the guardian replied. "You have the strength within you, Kael. It is not the power to wield a sword or cast magic that will define you, but the courage to face the darkness in your heart."

The creature stepped aside, revealing the stone altar behind it. The first shard of Illumina lay embedded in the stone, glowing with a brilliant light.

"Take it," the guardian said. "It is yours."

Kael stepped forward, heart pounding. He reached out and touched the shard. The familiar energy leapt into him, a surge of warmth and light. For the first time since leaving Rivenmere, Kael felt at peace. He had passed the test.

With a shimmer of its form, the guardian faded into the shadows, and the whispers became silence. Kael turned to Eryndor, who stood at the edge of the clearing, observing him with quiet pride.

"You did it," Eryndor said, his voice full of approval. "The first shard is ours."

Kael nodded, still shaken by the vision and the trial he had faced. He had claimed the shard, but he knew the road ahead would only grow more difficult.

They had merely taken the first step.

But on the path to stop the coming darkness, it was just the beginning.

# 3

# Journey to the Second Shard

The sun was setting as Kael and Eryndor left the Eldergrove behind. They had secured the first shard, but Kael knew their journey was far from over. The air was heavy with the weight of their mission, and with each passing step, his thoughts turned to the looming task ahead. The first shard had been difficult enough, and the trials he had faced had shaken him to his core. Yet, as they traveled further into the heart of the realm, Kael knew that the challenges would only grow greater.

"We've made good progress," Eryndor said, breaking the silence as they walked. His voice was low but steady, a reminder of the purpose that drove them both forward. "But there is much yet to do. The second shard lies to the north, beyond the Black Hills."

Kael turned to him, the familiar knot of uncertainty tightening in his chest. "The Black Hills? What's there? And how do we find the shard?"

Eryndor's eyes narrowed as he thought for a moment. "The Black Hills are a place of death and ruin. Many have tried to cross them, but few have returned. The land itself is cursed, haunted by the spirits of those who perished long ago. But beneath the cursed earth lies the second shard, guarded by a creature unlike anything we've encountered."

Kael shivered at the mention of that cursed land. He had heard of the Black Hills, tales of whispers spoken by villagers of strange lights and ghostly figures that wandered the hills at night. Still, he never imagined himself to be on a path that would lead him into their depths.

As if sensing Kael's discomfort, Eryndor continued, "Do not fear the Black Hills, Kael. We will be careful, and we will have the guidance of the shard you carry. It shall help us find our way."

Kael nodded, but he could not rid himself of the unease in his heart. The first shard had shown him that he was much stronger than he thought, but he was unsure whether this would be enough against what lay ahead. He was never a warrior, though he had strung up much in spirit; he knew not if he were ready for what lay beyond the Black Hills.

They pressed on in the wilderness, the forest gradually thinning as they made their way toward the mountains. The terrain became more rugged, and the air grew colder with the wind biting at their faces as it swept down from the higher altitudes. Longer days became much colder nights, yet still they pressed on, driven by the silent determination which, up until now, had hauled them along.

On the fifth day of travel from the Eldergrove, they arrived at the foot of the Black Hills. The scene before them was just as foreboding as Eryndor had described it: jagged and bare hills whose dark peaks rose towards the sky like the crooked fingers of some ancient creature; a desolate land with no life to behold. The ground was cracked and uneven, as if the earth itself had torn open during some cataclysmic event in ages past.

Eryndor paused at the edge of the hills, his gaze sweeping across the barren landscape. "This is it," he said softly. "We enter here, but we must be vigilant. The spirits of the fallen are restless, and the land itself is treacherous."

Kael swallowed hard. His throat felt dry. The air here felt heavier, different somehow-as if the very earth beneath his feet carried with it the weight of countless tragedies. He just couldn't shake this feeling that something was looking at them, sitting just out of the edge of his vision.

"How do we find the shard?" Kael asked, his voice firm despite his fear.

"The shard is concealed within the heart of the hills," Eryndor said. "It is on the Ruins of the Forgotten City, an ancient place lost to time. The city once flourished with a settlement, but was brought to ruin in a cataclysmic battle several centuries ago, and it is now a graveyard, haunted by the souls of those who fell in the fighting."

"And the guardian of it?" Kael asked, his heart pounding in his chest at the idea of facing another guardian.

Eryndor's face turned grave. "The guardian of the second shard is not a physical creature like that at the Eldergrove. It is an ethereal being-a manifestation of the spirits that haunt these hills. It will test our resolve, but unlike the first trial, this one shall be mental rather than physical. It shall seek to break us from within."

Kael nodded, taking Eryndor's words into his mind. Already the first shard had confronted him with more than he had thought he would have to face: his deepest fear. The mental trial ahead was something completely different, but he knew they did not have a choice. There was just too much at stake.

They entered the Black Hills, with its oppressive silence settling around them like a shroud. The path ahead was barely discernible, the ground uneven and treacherous. The deeper they proceeded into the hills, the heavier the atmosphere felt to Kael, who couldn't avoid the recurring thought that even the air was thick with the weight of too many lost souls. What had once been a lively land had turned into one filled with death, and it almost began to seem like its graveyard held more than just the bodies of the fallen.

It took a few days to cross the Black Hills, each day feeling longer than the last. Kael trekked across a barren landscape, where whispers in the wind grew soft and mournful to his ears, beckoning toward the darkness. Occasionally, when he turned his head, he thought he could make out the shapes of things moving just beyond his line of sight, shadowy figures that vanished the moment he turned his head. But when he told Eryndor about it, the mage dismissed him, saying that it was no more than hill spirits trying to drive them mad.

"Do not listen to them," Eryndor warned one night as they sat by their campfire. "These hills are filled with the voices of the lost, the ones who failed their trials long ago. They are not real, but they can still influence your mind. They will try to make you doubt yourself, to turn you against everything you believe in. But you must stay strong."

Kael nodded, but in his mind, there already clogged a multitude of doubts. What if the whispers were real? What if the spirits were trying to warn him—or worse, deceive him?

As the day wore on, and higher into the hills they climbed, the nature of the land began to shift. The ground grew uneven, rocky; rocks were everywhere and jagged and sharp. The sky above was grey and oppressive; light was filtered through thick clouds. It felt as though the very world was holding its breath, waiting for something to happen.

And then, as they reached the crest of the hill, Kael saw it.

In the distance, veiled by the maddening mists, were the ruins of an ancient city. Stone buildings had half-collapsed, their proud facades now disintegrating into dust. Jagged spires rose from the ruins like broken teeth, and the air around the city seemed to pulse with a strange energy. It was the Ruins of the Forgotten City—the heart of the Black Hills, and the place where the second shard lay hidden.

"We are close," Eryndor said, his voice level though the atmosphere was uncanny. "The shard is within the city, but the guardian shall not let us in without passing its trial."

Kael nodded, fortifying his spirit for what would be expected from him. They had gone this far, and now there was no going back.

As they entered the ruins, the whispers grew louder, more insistent. Kael's thoughts started to whirl and eddy, his doubts and fears rising within him like a tide. He felt a coldness creeping into his chest, a spreading sense of dread that threatened to consume him. The shadows seemed to move of their own accord, shifting in the corners of his vision. It was as if the ruins themselves were alive, watching, waiting.

And the trial had only just begun.

Suddenly, the earth beneath Kael's feet shook, and the air was alive with an eerie, otherworldly murmur. It was a voice-a soft voice at first, yet one that grew louder with each passing moment. The voice summoned him; it whispered his name, promised power, glory, and everything he had ever desired.

"Kael.," it whispered. "Come to me. all of your desires, all of your dreams, they can be yours. You need only embrace me."

Kael's heart raced within his chest. The voice was recognizable-too recogniz-able. It was his own, distorted by the darkness, promising so many seductive offers in an attempt to tempt him to take a course of ease.

But then, another voice cut through the darkness-a voice that was familiar, yet not his own.

"Kael, no! Don't listen to it!" It was Eryndor, an urgent strain in his voice.

The illusion shattered, and Kael found himself standing at the center of the ruins, breathing heavily, his mind struggling to clear the fog that had clouded it. The whispers fled, and the shadows fell back. The trial was over.

The second shard was within reach.

As Kael came up to the altar and the lying shard, the surge of power in his body grew. The trial had tested his mind, but now, the shard would test his heart.

The creature that had guarded it was gone, leaving only the pulsing light of the shard itself. Reaching out, the trembling of his hand slowly weaving into a fist, Kael grasped it.

The second shard was his.

But the journey was most certainly not at an end. The darkness was yet out there, and Kael knew that ahead lay trials far more hazardous than any he had thus far passed through.

And thus, with the second shard in hand, Kael and Eryndor again set their feet towards the unknown, knowing full well the fate of their world depended upon their shoulders.

The ride from the Black Hills proved to be far more hazardous than Kael had planned for. The weight of the second shard, now securely tucked away in his pack, felt like a constant reminder of the huge responsibility he was carrying. Despite defeating the guardian at the Ruins of the Forgotten City, the path ahead was anything but clear. Beyond the Black Hills, all was wild and unpredictable; it seemed even the forces of nature were against them as they worked their way toward their next destination.

Kael and Eryndor had been on the road for several days, each hour taking them deeper into a desolate landscape. A heavy fog filled the air, one that almost appeared to cloud their vision even. Gone was the familiarity of birds and animals making known their presence. It was as if the world itself had suddenly become quiet, anticipating something to happen. Each step they took seemed to have a tinge of apprehension-a silent sense of tension filled the air, like a storm cloud gathering but never breaking.

"We are nearing the border of the Shattered Lands," Eryndor said one evening as they camped under a canopy of gnarled trees. His voice was low, almost reverent. "This is the last known location of the third shard. But be warned, Kael. The trials here are unlike any we've faced before. They will test not just our bodies, but our hearts."

Kael nodded, the heaviness of Eryndor's words settling upon him. He had borne so much: bodily pain, mental torture, and the burden of failure and loss. Now, the trials would be more than simply battles or feats of determination-it would delve down into the very core of his soul, forcing him to confront the deepest parts of himself he had so long buried. He wasn't certain that he was ready for this, but he knew he couldn't turn back now. He had committed to this road and there was no turning back.

As they rode deeper into the Shattered Lands, the face of the land began to change. Trees grew twisted and blackened, their bark charred as if burned by some terrible fire. The earth was cracked and dry, with great furrows running along the ground. Above it, the sky was overcast all the time, a grey canopy that filtered the sun's rays into an unearthly, tinny light. The air itself seemed heavy with grief, as if the land itself was in mourning for some lost event.

When they finally reached the heart of the Shattered Lands, Kael was worn out, though it wasn't so much his physical body that felt strained but rather the tiring weight of his own mind. His head chugged with doubt and fear. What if he wasn't strong enough to face what trials waited ahead? What if he were to fail against the world and those who depended on him? His heart had already been tried in the fire of what he had endured in the Black Hills, but this... this was a whole different kettle of fish.

With night fully fallen, the uneasy silence of the land seemed to weigh even heavier. The wind tore through the gnarled trees, carrying with it whispers that seemed to be coming from every direction at once. Kael tried to ignore the voices, but they pressed against his thoughts like an invisible weight, tugging at his very soul.

"What is this place?" Kael asked, his voice barely above a whisper.

Eryndor spoke for the first time in most of their journey. "This was once a great kingdom, a place of prosperity and power. But greed and corruption took root here, and the land was shattered by the ambition of those who sought to control the very forces of life and death. The third shard lies deep within the ruins of the city that once stood here. But the price for obtaining it is high. The trials are not only physical but emotional. The heart is as vulnerable as the body, Kael. And this land preys on that vulnerability."

Kael shuddered, his mind folding in upon itself. He'd lost so much. He'd witnessed those close to him die, endured the cut of betrayal, and battled the unending darkness that appeared always to be lurking around the next bend. What if this test was the one he couldn't break?

They moved further into the ruins, the only sound being the crunch of their feet against the dry, brittle ground. An ancient city, once here, had long since crumbled into dust. The majestic buildings were little more than remains of what they had been. Shattered walls, columns, and fallen statues littered the barren landscape. It seemed even time had forgotten this place, leaving behind the faint whispers of a bygone era.

They were greeted by a large stone archway, with its once-proud pillars now crumbling with age at the center of the ruins. It was the entrance to the final trial, that gate leading to the third shard.

Kael's heart was racing in his chest as he stepped forward. It pressed down on him with the weight of this moment. The air grew heavier, thick with the power of ancient magic that still lingered in these ruins. As he passed beneath the archway, the earth beneath his feet seemed to shudder, and a low, rumbling sound echoed through the air.

The earth suddenly split in front of them, exposing a deep chasm. From within the recesses of the chasm, a figure began to rise–a figure cloaked in shadow, as if it took form from the darkness itself of the land. It was tall and imposing; its form indistinct, as if it were made from the very shadows that filled the air. Its eyes blazed with an unearthly light, fastening on Kael with a weight that burrowed into his marrow.

"You have come," the figure intoned. The voice echoed across the ruin. "But do you know what you seek? It would seem that what you want is before you, but first, you must show yourself worthy to take it. You have yet to face the trial of the heart."

Kael's breath caught in his throat. The trial of the heart? He thought he had faced such a trial already, back in the Black Hills, but this. this was something else altogether. The darkness that seemed to wrap around them like a shroud appeared to press in on him, and he could feel the weight of his fears and doubts rising within him, threatening to consume him.

The figure reached out with a ghostly hand, and a wave of energy washed over Kael, flooding his mind with images–flashes from his past, moments of weakness, pain, and regret. He saw his parents' death, his failures as a leader, the lives he had been unable to save. He saw himself in moments of cowardice, unable to act when it mattered most. The weight of those memories, those failures, crushed him, and in that instant, he felt the weight of the despair that once had almost destroyed him.

"Do you still wish to continue?" the figure asked, its voice soft and insidious. "You are not strong enough. You will fail, just as you have failed before."

Kael's knees buckled, and for one fleeting second, it was as if the darkness would consume him. Then, through his foggy memories, a shard of light pierced. Eryndor's words still lingered in his mind: The heart is as susceptible as the body.

Kael shut his eyes and drew deeply upon what little store of fortitude remained in him. He had confronted death before. He had stood on the brink of despair, and he had lived. He had endured. This was a trial no different, merely a test.

"I will not give up," Kael said, his voice shuddering but steady. "I will not let my past define me."

With these words, it seemed as if the shadows retreated, and the uncomfortable feeling of heaviness upon his shoulders began to lift. The figure standing before him suddenly wavered, its outline quivering like a mirage. Kael could feel the shard ahead of him, its pulse echoing through his chest, urging him forward.

The trial of the heart was not of the strength in the body, but in the strength of the spirit. He had looked into his fears, he had accepted his flaws, and yet he had refused to be broken by them. That was the true test, and he had survived.

The figure vanished, its form dissolving into the ether from which it had come. Lying before Kael was the third shard, its light now shining brightly, unhindered by the darkness which had surrounded it.

As Kael reached out to claim the shard, Eryndor appeared by his side. "You have done it, Kael. The third shard is yours."

Kael nodded, his heart still racing but filled with a sense of accomplishment. He was far from clear of the journey, but for the first time in a long while he felt that he might be able to face whatever came next.

They turned back together to the path ahead, knowing the darkness was not done with them. The final test lay still ahead, but they were closer to triumph. And in that instant, Kael knew whatever trials the future held, he would face them with a heart full of courage.

# 4

# The Gathering Storm

The wind had begun to shift, the air growing heavier with each passing hour as Kael and Eryndor made their way back from the Shattered Lands. The third shard was now safely tucked within Kael's pack, its energy pulsing steadily with the rhythm of his heartbeat. He felt its power, but he also felt the increasing weight of their mission pressing on him. The trial of the heart had been a harrowing experience, forcing Kael to confront his own deepest fears and regrets. Though he had emerged from the ordeal stronger, a part of him still wondered whether the challenges ahead would demand more than he could give.

Eryndor walked beside him, his usual quiet calm almost unsettling in light of the trials that had faced them. Kael had always admired the elven warrior's strength and resolve, but he couldn't shake the feeling that something had shifted between them. Eryndor had been steadfast, even he seeming to feel the looming weight of their task now. The land around them was becoming more ominous, the wilderness that was once pristine now shrouded in dark clouds, which hung low in the sky as though the heavens themselves were preparing for a storm.

"Do you feel that?" Kael asked, breaking the silence.

Eryndor nodded, his sharp eyes scanning the horizon. "The winds are shifting, and not to a direction we'd want. The darkness is stirring again. Something is coming."

Kael frowning tried to repress the growing sense of unease. The shards, the trials, all they had faced so far had only been the beginning. The true challenge still lay ahead, and he had a feeling that the storm Eryndor spoke of was only a foretaste of the coming battle.

As they continued through the thick woods that bordered the Shattered Lands, Kael couldn't help but notice how different the air had become. The world around them felt unnatural, increasingly so. The trees, once vibrantly alive, had become gnarled-twisted, their branches reaching out like grasping fingers of some sort. The ground beneath their feet was no longer solid but soft and treacherous, as if at any minute it might give way. Every sound was amplified, each step taken with the echo of a thousand unseen eyes watching from the shadows.

"This is not natural," Kael murmured; his senses were accentuated. "The land. it's dying."

"Aye," Eryndor said in agreement, his voice rare in its hint of sadness. "The Shattered Lands are but a symptom of a greater sickness, one that has spread across the world. The shards you seek-each one is a key to unraveling the curse that holds our lands captive. But the curse is not just in the land itself. It's in the hearts of men, in the darkness that festers within them."

Kael nodded, his thoughts chewing over the weight of Eryndor's words. He had known all along that the shards were important, but he had never truly realized just how grave their mission was. The curse, the suffering land, it was all connected. The shards weren't just relics of power; they were pieces of a puzzle that, once whole, could either save their world or utterly destroy it.

Their conversation was cut short as they reached a clearing; the ground here was strangely bereft of any greenery. In the middle of the clearing stood an ancient stone pedestal, worn by age but standing resolute. Resting atop the pedestal was one glowing object–the fourth shard.

It was different from the others. While the first three had been made from crystal and stone, this shard seemed to be forged from the very essence of the night sky. It shimmered with inky blackness, though with flashes of silver light streaking through it, like distant stars caught in the grasp of some unseen force.

"That's it," Kael whispered, stepping forward. "The fourth shard."

Eryndor's hand shot out, halting him. "Be careful, Kael. This shard is different from the others. It is not only a part of power but a test–a test of trust."

Kael looked into Eryndor and asked, "A test of trust?"

Eryndor's eyes were grave, his expression stern. "Yes. The fourth shard is bound by an ancient enchantment that will not allow it to be claimed by force. You must prove your worth, not through strength or battle, but through the trust of another. The shard will choose its bearer, and it will not accept you unless you are worthy of its power.

Kael swallowed, his nerves on edge. Trust? What did that even mean? He had trusted Eryndor and the others on this journey, but this felt different; he felt as though he were being asked to bare his soul–to expose vulnerabilities he had never shown to another before.

He took a deep breath and stepped toward the pedestal, reaching out with his hand. The instant his fingers came into contact with the shard, a surge of energy coursed through him, sending a wave of disorienting sensations cascading through his mind. He felt a cold, as if the deep chill of winter had settled over him, followed by a warmth, the sensation of standing in front of a crackling fire. The two sensations collided inside of him, and for a moment, he lost himself to the tide of emotions.

Suddenly he found himself standing in a darkened forest, alone. Above, the sky was swirling with storm clouds, thick with the promise of danger. From a distance, he heard voices-familiar voices-calling to him. He turned, his heart racing, but there was no one there.

"Kael!" The voice was echoing, distant but clear.

"Kael, you have to choose!"

He spun around, but the voices faded, replaced by a deep, resonating silence. A shadow flickered at the edge of his vision-something large, dark, threatening-moving swiftly through the trees. Panic surged within him, and he took off running, feet pounding against the forest floor.

The shadow followed.

"Kael!" The voice again, but this time it was different. It was a voice he had heard only once before—the voice of his sister, Lyra.

"Lyra!" Kael shouted, his breath coming in ragged gasps. But the shadow was too fast, too close. He could hear its breath now, deep and slow, like the growl of some great beast. He could feel its presence, its hunger.

"Kael, you got to believe me!" Lyra's voice cried out, but the words were drowned by the sound of the shadow's chase.

He turned again, desperation flooding his chest. And there, standing in the distance, he saw her- Lyra, in her outstretched arms, full of angst. "Believe me, Kael!" she screamed.

He was running, almost without thinking, toward her, the shadow hot on his heels. Yet the nearer he drew, the further she seemed to move, keeping her figure always just out of reach.

Kael's heart twisted in his chest as a storm of emotions battled within him. All his life, he had believed that trust was earned, a rare and precious thing. But here, now, he was being asked to trust implicitly, to leap into the void without knowing if he would be caught or left to fall.

The shadow reached for him, and in that instant, Kael made his decision. He closed his eyes, released his fear, and let himself trust.

The world exploded around him.

Kael gasped as his vision swam and he was yanked back into the clearing. The fourth shard was still in his hand, its surface now glowing with an ethereal light. He could feel its power coursing through him, its energy no longer cold and alien but warm, as if it had been waiting for him to accept it.

He looked up at Eryndor, concern etched upon his face. "You did it," the elf said, his voice soft with wonder. "You passed the trial. The shard has accepted you."

Kael's heart was still racing, his mind reeling from the intensity of the vision. The maelstrom of emotions that had assaulted him was overwhelming, but he had done it. He had trusted. The fourth shard was his.

As the light of the shard dimmed, Kael took a steadying breath. The trials were far from over. But he had learned something crucial today: Trust was not only a bond between people, but also a linkage to the world—a readiness to leap into the void and believe that something would catch him, even in those moments when the dark seemed to swallow all.

With the fourth shard now in his possession, Kael turned to Eryndor, his resolve strengthening. "Let's go," he said, his voice clear and determined. "We're not done yet."

The storm was gathering. And Kael knew, with each passing moment, that the true battle was only just beginning.

The journey had taken them farther from the familiar and deeper into the unknown. Every day it seemed, Kael felt that shards were growing heavier in his possession. Unlike all of these, the fourth shard had been claimed and yet its power was what left him ill at ease. It was not just an object of magical strength; rather, it was a force-a piece of the very fabric of the world itself-tied into the darkness they had long feared. The more he used it, the more he realized how dear a price that power came with.

Eryndor had watched always, seldom speaking since the fourth shard had been attained, but his silence spoke volumes of thought. Kael could feel the elven warrior's unease yet stoicism in Eryndor had always been a shield-a shield that in these darkening times seemed to grow thinner. Even the very land around them had grown more hostile since their departure from the Shattered Lands, it seemed. The forest was thickened, the trees taller and more twisted, their limbs grasping like skeletal fingers. And the further they pressed on, the more Kael felt them being drawn by some insidious pull toward something old and awful.

The mist came in off the hills, boiling around their legs like some hidden thing was breathing. It felt heavy, as if the world was holding its breath. Every noise muffled, every step a soft thud in the heavy silence. The scent of decay hung heavy on the wind, and Kael couldn't shake the feeling they were being watched.

"Do you feel it?" Kael whispered, his voice no louder than a gentle breeze, as if to speak louder would anger whatever was out there in the mist.

Eryndor's eyes narrowed, his gaze cutting through the horizon of mist. "Aye," he whispered, "it's near. Too near. Ahead of us is the Abyss."

Kael's heart raced at the mention of the Abyss. The legends spoke in hushed tones of it: an ancient chasm of darkness, where the very fabric of the world had been torn asunder. A place of great and terrible power, yet equally of unspeakable danger. It was said that only those who had truly lost themselves, who had given in to the lure of darkness, could survive its depths. For many who ventured into the Abyss, there was no return; if they returned, it was with their minds twisted by the things seen.

Eryndor led the way, his movements lithe and premeditated, as though each step had been conserved for this very moment. Kael followed closely, his hand resting on the hilt of his sword, even though he knew no blade would protect him from that which faced them. The fourth shard pulsed at his side–a constant reminder of unfinished business.

The mist deepened and closed in as they went on, till it appeared the world around them dissolved into a realm of shadowy shade. The ground under their feet grew rougher, jutting rocks tearing themselves from the earth as if the land itself was twisted from within by the power of the Abyss. It was then that Kael saw it—a great wall of stone rising before them, its surface slick with an unnatural sheen, reflecting no light. The Abyss had revealed itself in its true form, and its presence felt as though it were breathing, alive and hungry.

"We are here," Eryndor said, his voice low and tinged with something Kael couldn't quite place–fear, perhaps, or reverence. "The Gate of the Abyss."

Kael's heart was racing. The Gate was an ancient thing, built long before even the elves had walked the earth. It had been lost to time, hidden away in the forgotten corners of the world, and yet here it was standing before them. The gate itself was carved with intricate runes, symbols that Kael could not understand but which seemed to thrum with an energy all their own. It was as if the stone itself remembered—remembered ancient, forbidden memories—whispering their secrets to whoever would listen.

Eryndor stepped forward, his hand tracing the runes across the gate. This is where it all began. The Abyss was never a place of darkness. In times past, it was a crack between realms, a passage connecting the world of men to the Void, a place where everything lost was to be found. But it proved too tempting, too powerful. The ones who tried to subdue it were consumed by it, and in time, the Abyss became something far worse-something which devours not just the body but the soul itself.

Kael swallowed hard, the words of Eryndor weighing heavily upon him. He knew of the Abyss, of course, but to hear of it spoken so plainly made it all that much more real, that much more dangerous. His grasp on the shard at his side tightened.

"Why are we here?" Kael asked, trying to steady his breathing. "What is it that must be done?"

Eryndor faced him then, his gaze unyielding. It is the key to the Abyss-the fourth shard that must be placed within the Gate to open it, just as the other shards must be placed within their corresponding locations to unlock the other gates scattered across the world. For every puzzle part, there is one held by a gate. Not until all the shards are united shall we have the power to face this darkness that threatens to consume us.

They hung in the air-a promise and a curse at once. Kael knew that their journey wasn't just about collecting shards; it was about understanding the power they had and knowing when to use it and when to walk away.

He took a deep breath and stepped forward, his trembling hand reaching out for the fourth shard. He could feel its energy coursing through him, the weight of its power both exhilarating and terrifying. The instant his fingers touched the stone of the Gate, the air around them shifted. From deep within the earth, a low rumble echoed and the runes on the gate began to glow, their light casting eerie shadows on the rocks that surrounded them.

He could feel the Abyss, a deep, gnawing tug that pulled at the edges of his mind, begging him to step forward, to give in to the darkness. Kael clenched his jaw, fighting off its appeal, but the shard seemed to respond to the call, its energy surging more powerfully with each passing second.

"Now," Eryndor whispered, "place the shard."

For one long moment, Kael wavered, his heart racing. He didn't know what would happen once the shard was laid in place-whether it would open the gate or whether it would unleash something far worse. But he knew this was their only chance, the only way to move forward.

With a steady hand, Kael set the shard into the very center of the Gate. The world seemed to shift with a suddenness that belied its age, from the moment it touched. The ground at their feet shook, and a brilliant flash emanated from the runes, heading directly for the sky with an earsplitting scream. Kael fell backward, covering his eyes against the stark brightness, but he could not get away from it. The world seemed to tear at its seams, the very fabric of reality unraveling as the Gate began to open.

And then, as suddenly as it had begun, the light vanished. The roar faded, replaced by an eerie silence.

Kael opened his eyes, his breath catching in his throat. The Gate had opened, its gates torn wide, but it had not revealed the Abyss in full form. It was a rift-opened, swirling vortex of shadow and light, a vision of a world beyond their own. He could see flashes of landscapes-cities in ruin, mountains consumed by fire. He could hear screams, the sound of war, something darker still.

But it was not just a vision. It was a call, a summons.

Eryndor's voice broke the silence. "We are not alone."

Kael turned to see dark figures emerging from the shadows of the gate. They were cloaked in tattered robes, their faces hidden behind masks of bone and metal. Their presence was suffocating, as though they carried with them the weight of all the souls that had been lost to the Abyss.

"They are the Watchers of the Threshold," said Eryndor, his voice trembling with terror. "They bar the way in, that no one may pass in or out-but they are not of this world-they are the shades of those that fell to the darkness."

The Keepers moved closer, their eyes glowing with an unholy light. Kael could feel the heavy weight of their gaze upon him, as though they could see right into his very soul. He clutched his sword a little tighter, ready to defend himself at any moment, but Eryndor stepped forward, his hand raised in a gesture of peace.

"We seek only passage," Eryndor said, his voice almost calm, yet full of authority. "We seek to end the curse that binds our world, to avoid the ruin that will be. We do not come to conquer the Abyss-we come to seal it."

The Keepers were silent, and their presence grew heavier, their movements sluggish and premeditated. They did not come here to negotiate. They came here to judge.

The weight of the shards and the pressure of the Abyss started to bear down heavier upon Kael. A choice had to be made.

And the storm that had been gathering on the horizon had finally arrived.

# 5

# Battle for the Shards

The air was thick with tension, and Kael could feel the weight of the moment pressing on him like a physical force. The Keepers of the Gate were silent, their presence oppressive and unnerving, standing like statues with eyes that glowed with an unholy light. Their very existence felt like a reminder of all that had been lost to the Abyss, a warning of the doom that threatened to consume the world. Kael's heart pounded in his chest as he stood before them, the fourth shard still resting within the Gate, its dark energy swirling like a storm within him.

Eryndor stepped forward, his voice low and almost apologetic yet full of authority as he spoke to the Keepers. His voice was resolute but retained an undercurrent of desperation. They were not here to fight the Keepers; they were here to request a way into the Abyss, to find the other shards, to keep the end of all things from happening.

The Keepers were not here to negotiate, however. They showed no interest in understanding Kael and his companions desperate plight-they had only one purpose in mind: to protect the gate, guarding secrets that lay beyond. Too many had already fallen to darkness; they will not allow the living to undermine what had been done.

Kael's grip on his sword tightened. The shard at his side pulsed, its dark energy resonating with the growing tension in the air. He could feel the pull of the Abyss, as though it were calling to him, beckoning him to step forward, to embrace the darkness. But he fought against it. He had no intention of succumbing to the power of the Abyss. Not now, not ever. His mission was crystal clear: to protect the world, to stop the curse that threatened it.

The Keeper in the center, taller and more imposing than the others, took a step forward. Its eyes fastened on Kael with an intensity that made his skin crawl. The figure raised a skeletal hand, and the shadows around them seemed to deepen, swirling like a storm of darkness.

"You seek to enter the Abyss," the Keeper's voice boomed, a deep rumbling sound that seemed to reverberate through the very ground. "But you are unworthy. You are not ready to face what lies beyond. The shards you seek are not mere trinkets—they are pieces of a power that can unmake the world. The darkness is not a force to be wielded. It is a force that consumes all who dare to control it."

Kael took a step closer, his hand still firmly clenching his sword. "We aren't here to master the darkness. We are here to put an end to it. The Abyss has swallowed enough as it is. We must find the other shards and seal it away forever."

The Keeper's eyes narrowed, and the shadows around them thickened, pushing in on Kael and his companions. The air was suffocating, its weight almost unbearable. "You speak of sealing the Abyss," the Keeper said, its voice taut with disdain. "But the Abyss cannot be sealed. It is a part of the world. It always has been. You are fools to think you can erase it."

Eryndor stepped forward, his eyes ablaze with determinations. "We are not fools. We are the last hope of this world. If we do not succeed, everything falls to darkness; the Abyss will consume us all, and naught will be left."

The Keeper didn't say anything for a moment. He raised his hand, and the air crackled with dark energy around them. The shadows deepened and began to swirl in a violent dance across the walls, as if it had become alive from the command of the Keeper. The other Keepers stirred in agitation, shifting forms, growing liquid and perilous. They were no longer merely guardians of the gate but enemies unto themselves, protectors of a secret that the world could ill afford to keep.

In an instant, the air tore open in a light so brilliant that seemed to blind, and the Keepers charged. Their movements were swift and silent, like shadows come to life. Kael barely had time to react before the first Keeper lunged at him. Just in time, he raised his sword as the strike came, its force running through his body like a shockwave. Unbelievable strength; the Keeper's blade was like an extension of darkness itself.

Kael stumbled backward, catching his footing just in time. The Keeper's eyes shone with an unearthly light, while its grin was hidden behind a mask of bone. The air around them vibrated with dark energy; the very earth was shaking beneath their feet. Kael knew this was far from a normal fight. This was a fight for life–and for the end of the world.

"Stay close!" Eryndor shouted, his voice a command that cut through the chaos. "We must keep the shard safe!"

Kael nodded, his eyes locked upon the Keeper before him. He swung his sword, his blade slicing through the air with deadly precision. But the Keeper was faster, dodging the blow with supernatural agility. Kael was forced to parry another strike, the clash of their weapons ringing through the air like some kind of bell.

Eryndor was fighting another Keeper; his twin blades flashed in the poor light with the grace and precision common to elven kind. The elf warrior was a blur of motion: each strike calculated, each step deliberate. But even Eryndor's skill seemed to be tested by the unrelenting onslaught of the Keepers.

Kael felt the tension build, the weight of the battle pressing down on him with every passing moment. The shard pulsed at his side, its dark energy vibrating in response to the chaos around them. He could sense its power growing, as though it were feeding off the violence, feeding off the desperation. A tempting force, begging him to let go-to allow its power to overwhelm him. But Kael knew better than to give in. He had to stay focused. He had to survive.

As the battle raged on, Kael found himself hounded to the edge, his sword flashing through the air in a desperate attempt to keep the Keeper at bay. The Keeper was without quarter, brutal strikes not letting up, so he had to parry each one with an invariable shock that ran through his body. He felt his strength wane; his muscles were burning, his breathing short gasps, and yet he fought on.

Then, in the midst of all that chaos, something changed.

The shadows around them appeared to shift, the air growing colder, heavier. Kael felt a shiver run down his spine as, quite suddenly, the Keeper before him stopped. Its eyes, aglow with an unholy light, centered on something behind him. Kael turned in time to see Eryndor stumble, his movements slowing, his blades now slow in the air.

"Eryndor!" Kael yelled, a rising panic in his chest.

But the elf warrior could not answer. The Keeper's shadow had enveloped him, wrapping around him like some living thing, siphoning from him his very life force. Eryndor's face was pale now, his eyes wide with shock, as he struggled against the shadow's hold.

"No!" Kael roared, his heart racing. He ran to Eryndor's side, but the Keeper was before him, its hand out to stay him.

"You are too late," the Keeper said, his voice cold, final. "The darkness has already taken him, and you cannot save him."

Kael swung with all his force, but the Keeper's shadow absorbed the strike, the blade passing through the darkness like water. The Keeper's eyes gleamed bright with dark humour as he clutched at Eryndor.

Kael's breathing picked up as desperation was growing in his chest. He could not lose Eryndor. He could not lose anyone else. The weight of the mission, the weight of the world, pressed down on him, and he knew the only way to stop this madness was by ending the fight here and now.

Kael let out a defiant cry, hefting the sword high above his head, clutching tightly, eyes ablaze with fury. The shard at his side pulsed in response, dark energy surging through him and filling him with power unlike anything he had felt before. He could feel the darkness-the pull of the Abyss-but he resisted. This power was not his to command-but it could be used.

In one swift motion, Kael plunged his sword into the heart of the Keeper, the blade sinking deep into the darkness. The form of the Keeper rippled, as if made of smoke, and with a terrible scream, it disintegrated into nothingness, its shadowy tendrils unraveling.

With a crash, Eryndor fell to the floor, his body as limp as a wet towel, but still breathing. Kael rushed immediately to his side, his heart racing against his chest as he felt for a pulse.

"Eryndor?" Kael said in a low tone, shaking the elf's shoulder. "Eryndor, wake up."

The elf's eyes fluttered open, and he gasped for breath, his body trembling. "I... I thought it was too late," Eryndor whispered.

Kael helped him sit up, relief flooding through him. "It's not too late. We're not done yet."

But as Kael looked back at the Gate, he knew the battle was far from over. The Keepers had been defeated, but the darkness still lingered, its grip on the world tightening with every passing moment.

The war was just beginning.

The Gate was still. The battle had subsided, but the air hung thick with the remnants of dark energy. Kael stood at the edge of the ancient structure, his breath coming in short, ragged gasps. His body was battered, his muscles aching from the fierce combat; however, the real weight of the moment lay not in his physical exhaustion but in the great responsibility that now weighed upon his shoulders. The darkness had been beaten back, but only for a time. The war was far from won yet. There was no time to rejoice in the painful victory.

Eryndor stood beside him, his usually serenity-lined face clouded with weariness. His twin blades were still sheathed at his side, but the warrior's stance spoke of a man who had seen one time too many the cost of battle. Next to them, Alia and Rian were seeing to the wounded; their faces were etched with concern. Rian, the young healer who had, until now, kept them alive through the worst of the battle, was proving more capable than anyone could have hoped, but there was no telling how much longer they could continue without rest. The group had pushed forward with nothing more than their will to survive, but now, Kael knew, the real test would begin.

"We must go," Kael said in a low, grim tone. He looked down at the shard that hung from his belt; the dark energy still pulsed with its frightening rhythm. "The Keeper said the Abyss cannot be sealed. It's a part of the world. But if we don't find the remaining shards to complete the ritual, the darkness will consume everything."

Eryndor nodded, his eyes flicking to the shard at Kael's side. "The Keepers were right. The Abyss cannot be locked away. We can only delay it, contain it. But even that is a perilous task. The power we seek to control is not something that can be wielded lightly."

Kael grasped the shard, letting the chill of it seep into his palm, and nodded. "We don't have the time to spare. We have to find that last shard before it's too late."

Alia approached, her brow furrowed with concern. "We're all exhausted, Kael. We need rest. You're pushing us too hard."

"We don't have time for rest," Kael said; his tone was sharper than he had meant it to be. "If we don't get the last shard, it won't matter how much rest we get. We'll all be dead. This is bigger than all of us."

Rian, silent to this point, spoke her voice shaking, though resolute. "Kael's right. We don't know what's out there, or what the next trial will be. But if we stop now, if we let our guard down, we might never have a chance to finish this. We have to keep moving."

Eryndor laid a hand on Kael's shoulder, his face a mask of quiet understanding. "We all want to end this, Kael. But you cannot lead us into the next battle while we are broken. You've seen the way the darkness draws on your strength. The more you push yourself, the more the shard will consume you."

Kael closed his eyes for a moment, his grip tightening on the shard as he fought back the surging urge to embrace the power it promised. He knew they were right: he had already felt the pull of the Abyss, and with every step forward, it grew harder to resist. The shard's power was intoxicating-promising strength in exchange for his soul. But he couldn't afford to lose himself to it-not when so much was at stake.

"We'll take a short rest," Kael said finally, relenting. "But we move again at first light. We have no choice."

With that, the group made for shelter near the ruins of the Gate, a safe distance away from the crumbling structure. As night fell, the stars above twinkled in the vast expanse of the sky, and the group settled down, each lost in their own thoughts. Kael couldn't shake the feeling of impending doom that gnawed at him. Even while his body begged for rest, his mind refused to be still. He knew the last shard was close; he could feel it. He also knew that the true battle lay ahead. The shards were much more than simple objects of power, but keys to some sort of ancient, dark magic that none could truly comprehend. And with each shard they collected, the cost grew greater and greater.

Kael lay awake, staring at the flickering campfire well into the night. Eryndor had succumbed to a fitful sleep, his breathing low and even, but Kael's mind could not quiet. He needed answers. He needed to understand the power of the shards and why they were so dangerous. The Keepers had warned them, but they hadn't shared enough to truly prepare them for what lay ahead.

As suddenly, a soft voice whispered beside him.

"Kael?"

He looked to see Alia standing over him, her face pale but set. She'd always been the one to speak truth when speaking it was hard to hear.

"I've been thinking about what the Keeper said," she said, her voice barely more than a whisper. "About the Abyss being part of the world, something we can't seal. What if it's not just some force we need to stop? What if it is something we are meant to understand, something we need to know how to control?

Kael sat up, furrowing his brow. "Control the Abyss? You mean, we should use the shards for our own benefit?"

Alia shook her head. Her face was thoughtful. "No, not for our own benefit. Still, if the Abyss truly is part of the world, then perhaps there's a way to learn to coexist with it-to harness its power without its overpowering us."

Kael's heart was racing. The thought was a dangerous one, yet something about the way she said it resonated. "You think we could control the Abyss? With the shards?"

Alia glanced down at the ground and then back up at Kael. "I don't know. But I believe we have to learn more. We have to understand the power we're dealing with before we allow it to control us."

But before Kael could say anything, a loud rustling interrupted them. Rian, who was standing a little aside, moved closer, her face tense.

"They're coming," she said, her voice firm though her eyes betrayed her fear. "The last shard is close by, but so are the others who seek it."

Kael stood, his sword drawn in an instant, his senses on high alert. "We knew this would happen," he muttered. "We can't let anyone else get to the shard first."

Eryndor was already awake, his blades drawn and ready for combat. "We must move quickly. The last shard lies in the Tomb of the Forsaken, and we're not the only ones who know of its power."

The group gathered their belongings quickly, preparing to leave before their pursuers arrived. Kael couldn't shake the feeling that they were being hunted—not just by the forces of darkness, but by something far worse: an ancient order that had long been waiting for this moment.

As they trekked toward the Tomb of the Forsaken, the shadows of the night grew darker, and the sense of foreboding intensified. The wind howled through the trees, a lamenting cry as if the very world were warning them of the terrors ahead. Kael knew that there was one final test ahead of them and that they would be expected to take it together. But he also knew that not all of them would emerge alive. The shards were too powerful, and the darkness too strong.

Before them stood the Tomb of the Forsaken, an ancient structure half-buried into the earth, its entrance a yawning mouth that seemed to drink in all the light that shone upon it, Kael took a great breath, his heart pounding in his chest. Here it was. The last shard awaited them. But accompanying it came the promise of a battle unlike anything they had ever fought.

As they neared the entrance, Kael met Eryndor's gaze and saw in his eyes the silent acknowledgment. This was the moment. Whatever was to come next, together they would face it.

And then, as they stepped into the darkness of the tomb, the world shifted, and the final battle for the shards began.

# 6

# The Tomb of Forsaken Secrets

The entrance to the Tomb of the Forsaken was an ominous sight. Its towering stone walls were etched with ancient symbols, some worn away by centuries of neglect, others glowing faintly as if infused with the essence of forgotten gods. The air around it seemed to hum, thick with a palpable energy, as if the very tomb itself were alive. Kael, Eryndor, Alia, Rian, and the others stood before it, unsure of what they would find within its dark depths. The wind whistled eerily through the cracks in the stone, whispering of the dangers that awaited them inside.

Kael's heart raced as he peered into the darkness that beckoned from beyond the threshold. It was inside, and it was the last shard—the one that could save or destroy the world—and it was just a question of time before the others, those that sought shards for what was in it for them, arrived. Kael fisted his hand at his side around the shard, feeling the dark energy coursing through him. A gift-a curse. If he wasn't careful, it would overwhelm him.

"We can't wait any more," Kael said, his voice firm. "We have to get inside before the others do."

Alia stepped forward, her brow furrowed in concern. "What if this is some sort of trap? The tomb may be rigged with spells, or worse-things that will guard the shard.

Eryndor nodded. "The Tomb of the Forsaken was never meant to be explored by anyone. Its defenses are likely more dangerous than anything we've faced so far."

Kael met Eryndor's gaze, his eyes hard with resolve. "It's too late to turn back. The Abyss is coming, and we either stop it now or lose everything.

Until now, Rian had been silent, but he spoke now, his voice low. "We can't let fear stop us now. We've made it this far, and if we stop now, we'll only doom ourselves."

Kael nodded sharply. "Let's go."

With that, they stepped forward, crossing the threshold and entering the tomb. The air inside was cold and heavy, carrying on it the scent of ancient stone and dust. The light from their torches danced across the walls in long, twisting shadows, adding to the sense of disquiet. The passage unfolded before them, dark and forbidding, yet Kael's instincts pushed him onward. He could feel the shard's power drawing on him, urging him deeper into the heart of the tomb.

The deeper they ventured, the more the tomb seemed to shift around them. The stone walls seemed to grow more oppressive, the passage narrowing as if it would swallow them whole. The ground beneath their feet was uneven, and the path was littered with ancient bones, relics of those who had come before them. Some of the bones were too well-preserved, too fresh in appearance, as though they had only been there a matter of days. Kael looked at Eryndor, who nodded silently. They were not alone.

"There's something here with us," Eryndor whispered, his voice low and even. His senses were honed from years of battle, and he could feel the disturbance in the air as well.

Kael didn't respond, but his grip on his sword tightened. He wasn't afraid—not yet—but the feeling of being watched, of something lurking just beyond the reach of their light, was unsettling.

They entered a huge chamber where the ceiling disappeared upwards into the darkness. An altar stood in the center of the room, old and overgrown with moss and dust. On top of it was one single object: a black stone pedestal holding the last shard. It glowed softly, pulsating as if in time with Kael's heartbeat.

"That's it," Kael whispered, going to the pedestal.

But before he could reach it, a low growl resounded through the chamber, followed by the scraping of stone upon stone. From the shadows, enormous shapes began to emerge; creatures of bone and shadow were those, their eyes glowing with malevolent light. They were the Guardians of the Tomb, ancient protectors tasked with the duty of ensuring that no one, not even the most noble of souls, could claim the power hidden within.

Eryndor's twin blades materialized in his hands in one swift motion, gleaming in the flickering light of the torches. "Prepare yourselves!" he yelled.

The creatures moved closer to them, their movements slow but calculated, eyes fixed on their intruders. Alia drew back her bow, nocking an arrow in place, as Rian sidled up beside Kael, her staff aglow with spells of healing as she stood ready to defend them.

Kael took a deep breath and, with a forceful motion, unsheathed his sword. The shard at his belt pulsed in time with the creatures' growls, urging him forward. But Kael hesitated. There was something strange in the air, something almost... familiar.

"I don't think we're meant to fight these creatures," Kael said, his voice uncertain. "They're not like the others we've faced."

Alia looked sideways at him, her eyes narrowing. "What do you mean?"

Kael forward, his sword lowered. "They're not attacking us out of malice. They're guarding something. But they're not the true enemy. The real danger lies in the tomb itself."

Eryndor's gaze turned from the creatures to Kael. "What are you saying?"

I think these Guardians are the protectors of the tomb," Kael said. "They're here to keep us from claiming the shard, but I don't think we have to fight them. We need to prove ourselves worthy of the power they guard.

The Guardians stopped, their radiant eyes fixed on Kael. For a long time, the space between them was thick with tense anticipation. Then, one of the creatures-the biggest among them-took another step forward, his face utterly empty of anything resembling emotion. He spoke, the sound of his voice, from deep within the tomb, ancient and heavy with power.

"You seek the shard," it said in a voice like dry leaves in the wind. "But you are not ready. The Abyss will consume you all. Only those who prove their worth may claim the power you seek. You must face the trials of the Forsaken."

Kael's heart missed a beat. "What trials? We've faced more than enough.

The tomb has many secrets," the Guardian intoned. "And only those who understand the darkness will be allowed to wield its power. You shall have to face your most horrible fears and confront a truth about yourselves.

The room seemed to darken as the Guardian's words echoed in the chamber. A sudden coldness swept over Kael, and the ground beneath his feet seemed to shift, as if the tomb itself were preparing to test them. The air grew heavy with magic, and Kael's grip on his sword tightened.

"I'm ready," Kael said, his voice firm. "We're ready."

The Guardian nodded, the joints creaking in a bone-aching sound. "Very well. The trials begin."

Before Kael could even react, the world changed around him. The shadows darkened, and the ground shook under his feet. The room spun, and the air turgid with fear congealed around him. Kael blinked, finding himself standing alone amidst an impenetrable darkness.

The breath caught in his throat as the familiar weight of the shard at his side pulsed in rhythm with the beating of his heart. "What is this?" he muttered to himself.

From behind him, a voice called–a voice he knew well.

"Kael."

He spun, his heart racing. "Mother?" The voice was unmistakable–his mother's voice, soft and full of love.

"Kael, my son. You've come so far," the voice continued to say, drawing closer. "But you cannot escape your past."

Kael's stomach twisted. His mother had died years ago, taken by the very darkness they now sought to defeat. She had died in his arms, her last words urging him to be strong, to protect the world from the forces of evil. But now, standing in the dark, it was as though she were right there with him, alive, waiting to speak to him once again.

"No," Kael whispered, his hands shaking as he reached out. "You're not real. You're part of the trial, aren't you?"

Her voice softened. "You never forgave yourself, Kael. You blamed yourself for my death, even though it was not your fault. But you must forgive yourself now, or the darkness will consume you as it consumed me."

Tears welled in Kael's eyes as memories of his mother flooded back—her smile, her warmth, her gentle guidance. He had blamed himself for her death, for not being able to save her, even though there was nothing he could have done. The guilt had haunted him for years.

But now, in the darkness of the tomb, he realized the truth.

"I forgive you, Mother," Kael whispered, his voice breaking. "I forgive myself."

The darkness receded, and the light returned. The trial was over, and Kael stood alone once more, his heart lighter than it had been in years. The vision of his mother had been a test, a way for him to confront his own guilt and find the strength to move forward.

The Guardian's voice once more boomed in the chamber. "You have passed the first trial. Now, the final test awaits."

Kael stepped forward, determination in his step. He was ready to face whatever lay ahead. The shard was within reach, and he was prepared to do whatever it took to claim it-and to save the world from the coming darkness.

The battle was far from over.

The air in the tomb grew colder, still, as Kael stood before the pedestal once more alone. The soft pulse of the shard at his side reminded him of the task at hand. The first trial was done, tiring and emotional, but it was done. Kael knew, deep in his bones, that the hardest challenge was yet to come. The trials of the Forsaken were far from over.

He turned back toward the entrance where the Guardians still stood in silent watch, their hollow eyes aglow faintly in the dim light of the chamber. Their form was unnatural; their presence a grim reminder of the powers of old that guarded this sanctum. Their warning was crystal clear: only those who were worthy could lay claim to the shard which lay ahead.

Kael's thoughts went back to the words of the Guardian: the tests within the tomb were not only physical but of the mind, spirit, and emotion. He had already faced his guilt-his unresolved feelings about his mother's death. Now he couldn't help but wonder what the next test would bring to surface. What darkness in himself would he face?

His fingers brushed the hilt of his sword, but he did not draw it. Instead, he approached the pedestal-where waited the final shard, glowing faintly with the power of ages past. The shard seemed to hum in time with his heartbeat, as though recognizing his presence. It was as if the very essence of the tomb was alive, aware of his every thought, every breath.

Kael did not hesitate but reached out for the shard. In that instant, his fingers touched its surface, and a blinding light erupted from inside the stone, filling everything around. The light enveloped him in a force so strong that it was if the very soul was being torn out.

But Kael did not flinch. He stood tall, determined. This was his moment.

Suddenly, the light vanished, and the tomb fell into absolute darkness. Kael could no longer see his hand before his face. His senses were overwhelmed, and for a moment, he felt disoriented, as if he were lost in a sea of shadows.

Then, a voice—low and menacing—whispered through the darkness. "You seek the power of the Abyss. But do you truly understand what it will cost you?"

Kael's heart skipped a beat. The voice was unfamiliar, but it carried an aura of ancient malice. It reverberated within him, as though it were speaking directly to his deepest fears.

"I don't seek power," Kael answered, his voice steady. "I seek to stop the darkness that threatens this world.

The voice laughed, a hollow echoing sound that seemed to come from all directions. "The darkness is within you. Do you truly believe you can stop it? You cannot fight what you are, Kael. You cannot escape your destiny."

Suddenly, a vision danced in front of Kael's eyes: his past–utterly real to him. The death of his mother, the inability to save his own people, so many battles having been fought, so many lives taken, so many that he had failed to save. His regrets crowded in around him, It felt as if his chest was going to cave in, and Kael almost believed that he would break down under the pressure.

But then the vision shifted. The weight of his past, his mistakes, the burdens of his soul fell away, like shackles, to reveal instead an overwhelming sense of power: dark, irresistible power. The shard pulsed at his side, and Kael felt its energy run riot through him, filling the void left by his grief, his guilt, his fears.

"You are nothing without it," the voice continued. "You are nothing without the power of the Abyss. Embrace it. Accept it. Become the one you were always meant to be."

The temptation was strong, for he had just spent so much of his life fighting to be something more, to protect the people he loves. The power was right there, within reach, and it could give him everything he ever wanted.

But Kael hesitated. He remembered what he had fought for, the reasons behind his journey. He had fought for his people, for the future, for those who could not fight for themselves. This power-this dark energy-it was not for him. He could not allow it to consume him, as so many before him.

"No," Kael whispered. "I won't let it control me. I choose to fight."

The vision of darkness receded; the voice fell silent. Kael's body shook, but he stood firm, his sword still in hand, his resolution unbroken. He had passed the second trial, the trial of temptation, and he would not let the power of the Abyss shape his destiny.

The tomb shook, even the ground beneath him trembling as the shadows retreated once more to reveal the shard's faint glow. This time, without any hesitation, Kael reached forward and picked up the shard from the pedestal. The darkness that had so nearly consumed him was conquered, but Kael knew the final trial was yet to come.

He turned back towards the Guardians and found them regarding him with eyes that were both unnerving and unblinking. Their skeletal faces were unreadable, but Kael felt a sense of approval in their gaze. The trial was not over, but he had proved his strength. He had resisted the darkness and its seduction, and now only one challenge remained.

The largest of the Guardians moved towards him; its hollow gaze fixed on Kael. "You have passed the trials of the Forsaken," it intoned. "But there is one final test. The power you now possess is not for the weak. It is a weapon, a tool, and it can either save the world or destroy it. The choice is yours. The darkness has claimed many before you, and now you must decide whether you will be its master or slave.

Kael stood tall, his fingers wrapped tightly around the shard. He could feel its power humming within him, in tune with his own energy. The final test was one of choices-a choice he had already made very long ago.

I will master it," Kael declared, his voice not wavered. "I will use its power to protect, to fight for the future. The darkness will not control me. I'll control it.

The Guardian's gaze softened, just slightly as if in recognition of Kael's resolve. "You have passed the final test, Kael of the Lightbringers. The shard is yours. But remember this-its power is not infinite. It is but a fragment of the whole, and there are those who would use it for their own ends. You are not alone in your journey."

With that said, the Guardians stepped aside; in a blink of an eye, the haunting figures faded into the dark recesses of the tomb. The air seemed to clear, and heavy weight that had filled the chamber lifted, revealing only the soft hum of energy emanating from the shard. Kael stood alone before the pedestal, his racing heartbeat now mixed with triumph and fear.

The shard was his.

But at what cost?

As he turned to leave, Kael knew the road forward would be a dangerous one. He had claimed the shard, but not everyone shared his ambition for its power. Others would come, and they would stop at nothing until it was taken from him. The Abyss would not be silenced so easily.

As Kael turned back through the tomb, he found that the walls around him were shifting as if the stone itself were alive. He felt the weight of the power he now possessed; however, he knew he was not alone. His companions awaited him-Alia, Eryndor, Rian-and together they were prepared to face whatever darkness lay in store.

The tomb behind him shut with an eerie finality, the entrance sealing itself shut. Kael could not help a pang of loss, though the shard was now in his hands-highway to nowhere, far from over. And as he stepped into the light, it seemed heavier than at any time in history. The power he held could save them all, or destroy everything they fought for. And the choice, as always, was his.

# 7

# The Last Convergence

The morning after Kael retrieved the shard, the world seemed quieter. The land around the tomb stretched far and wide, and the forests that once seemed so imposing were now nothing more than quiet witnesses to the unfolding journey. Kael stood at the edge of the forest, his eyes narrowing as he gazed at the horizon. The weight of the shard, still safely tucked within his pack, seemed to anchor him to the earth, yet the burden it carried was becoming more apparent by the minute. He could feel the pulse of its power, a steady rhythm that echoed his heartbeat.

It had been days since he left the tomb behind, yet the memories of his time within those forsaken walls were still fresh. Trials, darkness, and the whispers are clutched to him like a second skin that seemed to remind him of the cost for their victory. Kael had completed his set tasks, but there was no triumph within his heart. The trials tested his resolve, but surely hadn't prepared him for what would come. The final battle was on the horizon, and he wasn't sure he was ready.

His mind wandered back to his friends: Alia, Eryndor, Rian. Each had fought alongside him, each had struggled in their own ways, and each had made it through. But this-the final trial, the true test of strength-was different. The shard he carried was not just an implement; it was a key, a beacon that would lead the way but also signal the beginning of the end. The darkness was to come, and nothing would stand in its way to take the shard for itself.

Kael turned, his gaze lingering on the others who had assembled here in the clearing. Alia, ever the silent strategist, stood with her back against the trees, her eyes closed in contemplation. Eryndor, his once bright eyes now dulled with the shadows of battle, whetted his sword against the stump of an old oak. Rian was already off towards the horses, prepared to go at a moment's notice. All of them had changed, grown in ways Kael no longer could understand. They had all become more than just friends; they had become his greatest allies, and he could not afford to lose any.

She turned as he stepped forward, the dark eyes meeting his. There was nothing that needed to be said; she could see the weight on his shoulders, the struggle within him. She knew the shard's power better than anyone.

"Kael," she began softly, the weight of unsaid words carried in her voice. "The time is near. We must find the others.

Kael nodded, his expression grave. "I know. The trials are over, but the war is just beginning."

Rian looked over, raising an eyebrow. "So, we're just going to march right into the heart of this mess, aren't we? No more hiding, no more waiting."

Eryndor rose, standing tall as his hand closed tighter around the sword. "There is no more choice. The enemy comes. The power of the Abyss would not be refused. We have to take our stand."

Kael met Eryndor's gaze, saw the fire in his eyes, that unyielding determination which had been constant in their journey. Yet, Kael knew more than anyone that determination alone would not suffice. These enemies they were about to confront were far stronger than anything they had ever confronted.

"I do not know if we can win this fight," Kael said in a quiet voice. "The power we're facing—it's not like anything we've seen. It's not just armies or creatures. It's something more."

Alia stepped closer, her voice calm but firm. "Then we must stand together. We have come this far, Kael. We have seen what happens when we give in to fear. We have lost enough already. We cannot let that happen again.

Kael's gaze softened as he looked at her. She had always been the anchor, the voice of reason. It was her strength that had helped him through his darkest moments. He reached out, placing a hand on her shoulder. "I know. I'm just... not sure if I'm ready for what's coming."

They had all stopped talking and stood in silent contemplation, their own mind consumed by various thoughts. The road ahead would be long and very dangerous, but they had no other choice than to press on. They had come so far, and they would not turn back.

The journey to find the others was long and arduous, the land between the tomb and the city of Sarnoth vast with treacherous terrain, twisting rivers, and forests heavy with shadow. When the sun dipped below the horizon, the group made their camp near a small stream. The fire, crackling warmly, gave light, but did little for the sense of unease that hung over them.

Kael stared into the fire, his mind racing. He had no answers, no solutions. The darkness he had fought so hard to contain was growing stronger with each passing day. And now, the shard he carried-the power that had been gifted to him-was both a blessing and a curse. He could feel its power, its call, like a constant hum beneath his skin. It was not something he could ignore.

Alia sat beside him, her gaze strayed. "You're troubled," she said softly. "The shard. it calls to you, doesn't it?"

Kael looked up at her, suddenly appalled. "How did you know?

She smiled wistfully. "I have seen it before. The burden of power is weighty. You cannot bear it without it changing you. Yet you must also remember why you're doing this, Kael. The power isn't for you - it's for everyone else. You carry its burden for those who cannot.

He breathed out slowly, his fingers tautening around the shard in his pack. "I know. But sometimes, I wonder if I'm strong enough to bear it."

"You don't have to be strong alone," she replied softly. "We're all here with you. Don't forget that."

Kael nodded, her words anchoring him to the moment. He was not alone. Together they would fight, like they had from the start.

The others sat across from them, Rian and Eryndor talking in hushed tones as the fire crackled. Kael couldn't hear the specifics of their conversation, but every so often, a glance in his direction told him they were aware of his inward struggle. They, too, had seen what this journey had done to him. He was their leader, their guide, but Kael knew that in the end, it was their unity, their combined strength, that would see them through.

After some time, Eryndor finally spoke. "Tomorrow, we head to Sarnoth. The city's walls are the last line of defense against the Abyss. We cannot delay any longer."

Kael looked at him, nodding once more. "We leave at first light."

The night was spent in awkward silence, each man lost in his own thought. The fire burned low, the stars above flickering like the dying embers of some long-forgotten dream. Kael closed his eyes, but sleep was slow in coming. He could still feel the pulse of the shard beneath his skin, thrumming with an energy both comforting and terrifying.

They had packed up in the morning and headed out, taking the circuitous path in the direction of Sarnoth. Travel was hard, over rough and capricious land, yet Kael discovered that he felt focused now, propelled forward by a sense of determination he hadn't known in days. He could no longer doubt that this shard was here, and as they traveled deeper into the area, Kael felt its presence increasingly intertwined into his body.

It wasn't long before the city gates of Sarnoth came into view. Before them stood an ancient wall, tall and imposing; its stone surfaces had been weathered by countless seasons and wars. Kael could feel the weight of history pressing down upon them as they crossed the threshold. The city pulsed alive with activity, a bustling heart of traders and travelers alike, with lines of soldiers preparing for war. This was the last bastion of hope, the final place where they might rally their forces.

But Kael knew in his heart of hearts, the true battle was just beginning.

The gates of Sarnoth clanged shut behind them with a heavy, terminal clang, the sound reverberating off the stone walls of the ancient city. And Kael felt the weight of it—the finality of it all. They had come so far, endured so much, and now they were here, within the heart of the last stronghold against the Abyss. Many sieges had Sarnoth withstood, but it was not to be the same this time. This was an enemy like none they had known, and not even the walls of the city would hold for them forever.

Kael stood at the edge of the city, his eyes scanning the horizon. He could see the vast plains stretching out before him, dotted with forests and scattered villages. Beyond that, the mountains loomed, their jagged peaks piercing the sky. But it wasn't the landscape that held his attention-it was the sense of looming danger. The enemy was already out there, gathering in the shadows, waiting for the right moment to strike.

His thoughts were cut short by the sound of footsteps approaching. Alia, always so calm and collected, came to a stop beside him, her face grave. "Kael," she said quietly, her tone reflective of the weight that had begun to settle on all of them. "We can't wait any longer. The time has come. We must make our stand."

Kael nodded, his features hardening. "I know. But I don't think we're ready. The shard—

"Kael," Alia interrupted, her hand resting gently on his shoulder. "We've all seen what the shard can do. We've seen what it's capable of. But it's not the shard that will win this battle. It's us. It's the strength we've found in each other."

Kael turned to her, meeting her gaze. There was no fear in them, only resolution. That same resolution that had carried them through countless trials, that had held them together when everything seemed lost. Alia had always been the heart of their group, the one who knew how to lift their spirits when darkness seemed so overwhelming. And now, more than ever, they needed her strength.

"You're right," Kael said his voice evening out. "We have come this far together; we are stronger than we think."

They walked together down the streets of Sarnoth, the teeming city now filled with the silence of tension. People went about their duties, but one could not mistake the hint of fear that danced across the crowds. News of the enemy's advance reached every corner of the city, and the people knew what was to be expected. It was only a question of time before the walls would be tested.

As they reached the middle of the city, Kael saw the familiar faces of his companions: Eryndor and Rian and several others from their ever-growing alliance. They were converging near the great hall, where all the city leaders had summoned those who would stand against the Abyss.

Rian's eyes met Kael's, and he gave a grim nod. "We're ready," he said, his voice low. "But I don't know how much longer we can hold out. The enemy is closer than we thought.

Eryndor's face was grim as he added, "We will hold them off as long as we can, but this will be a battle like none we have ever faced. The forces of the Abyss are unlike anything we have come up against. They are relentless.

Kael looked to the assembled warriors, their faces a mixture of fear and determination. They were not seasoned soldiers, but they had something far more important-hearts. Each of them had fought alongside Kael and his companions through the darkest of times, and now they were ready to face the end.

What's the plan?" Kael asked, his eyes turning to the council of leaders who sat gathered in the hall. Their faces were somber, weighed heavy with their responsibilities. The leader of the council, a grizzled old man by the name of Boric, glanced up from the map that was spread out before him.

We've gathered every available soldier," Boric said, his voice rough with age. "But it is not enough. The Abyss is too powerful. We can only hope to hold the line long enough for the shard to do its work.

Kael frowned. "The shard alone won't be enough. We need more than just its power. We need to fight together. We need to rally every last person who is willing to stand with us."

Boric nodded gravely. "That's true, but the time is short. The forces of the Abyss are marching on us, and we must act quickly.

The council droned on, elaborating tactics, but Kael's attention would not be bound. His mind wandered back and again to the shard, concealed beneath his mantle. It hummed with power, its energy quivering in his breast. He could feel its presence, its need to be used. It was if the shard itself called to him, begging him to unleash its power upon the world.

Alia noticed that Kael had become distracted and walked up to him. "You're thinking about the shard again, aren't you?" she asked softly.

Kael nodded. "I can feel it. It wants to be used. But I'm not sure I can control it. What if—what if I make a mistake?"

"You won't," Alia said with emphasis. "We have all seen what you are capable of. The shard isn't just about power, Kael. It's about the will to use it in the right way. You have that will. Trust yourself."

Kael looked into her eyes, seeking reassurance. And in that moment, he knew it wasn't the shard he needed to have faith in, but his friends, his allies. Time and again, together they had faced impossible odds and emerged stronger every time. Now was no different.

"We fight together," Kael said, his voice level. "We win together."

With the final touches, the sun began to set, casting long shadows over the city. The air grew cold as the wind whispered through the streets, its softness carrying the faint scent of dust and smoke. The people of Sarnoth gathered in the square, their faces full of fear but somehow determination. It was time. The last stand was upon them.

Kael and his companions stood at the front of the assembled warriors, ready to lead the charge. The sound of marching feet filled the air as the soldiers took their positions along the city walls, their weapons gleaming in the fading light. Final instructions were given by the leaders of the city, and Kael felt the weight of their trust fall onto his shoulders. He was the one they had chosen to lead them, to wield the shard, to confront the enemy.

The ground beneath their feet began to shudder, and Kael's heart skipped a beat. Here came the Abyss.

A dark shadow loomed over the horizon, blotting out the stars as the first wave of the enemy emerged from the forests and hills. The army of the Abyss was great in number, beings of nightmare, warped by dark magic and unholy power. Their eyes pulsed with malignant energy; their footsteps rumbled like thunder as they churned towards the walls of Sarnoth.

Kael's hand tightened around the shard. In return, it pulsed in his hand-as if the shard, too, wanted to unleash its energy. But he knew he had to wait. The time for recklessness was over. He had to be precise. He had to use the shard when it mattered most.

The enemy charged, their dark energy piling up like a tsunami that broke against the defenses of the city. The first line of warriors met them with clashing steel, but it was an ominous portent: by all appearances, the odds were against them. Kael could feel the tension building in the air, the churning energy of battle mixing with the shard's power. It was time.

With a yell, Kael raised the shard high above his head; its energy poured into him like a rushing stream. The world around him seemed to slow down-the roar of the battle faded as he focused all his energy on the shard. The air crackled with electricity around him as the shard started to glow, its light tearing through the darkness like a beacon.

The enemy wavered, for one instant stunned by the raw power emanating from the shard. This was their chance, Kael realized. With a shout of resolve, he let loose with the shard, and an immoderate wave of energy rolled across the battlefield.

It was like no other blast they had ever seen. With piercing movements, the arc tore across the enemy lines, disintegrating creatures in its wake. The Abyss recoiled, its forces shattered by the naked force of Kael's attack. But it was a success that lasted only so long. The enemy was not that easy to be defeated.

From the very center of darkness, something big emerged–fearsome, shrouded in tatters, its eyes blazing with malevolent fire. The leader of the Abyss.

Kael's heart skipped a beat. Here was the acid test.

# 8

# The Darkening Hour

The air was thick with smoke, and the skies overhead were tainted a deep, oppressive red. The battlefield lay silent for a moment, as if the world itself was holding its breath. Kael stood amidst the chaos, his chest rising and falling with each ragged breath. The battle had been raging for hours, and despite their best efforts, Sarnoth's defenses were slowly but surely being breached. The enemy was relentless—creatures from the Abyss, monstrous and nightmarish, pushing ever forward with a single purpose: to wipe out the last remnants of humanity.

He could feel the pulse of the shard within him, humming with an insatiable hunger to destroy. Already, he had unleashed its power, tearing swathes through the ranks of the enemy army. Yet even the shard's overwhelming force could not stem the tide that rose against them. More and more creatures kept pouring in through the breaches in the walls, as if the very earth itself was giving birth to them. And there was no end to their numbers.

A strident cry rent the air as one of the nearby warriors went down, his life snuffed out in a swift, brutal moment beneath the claws of a shadow beast. Kael's grip tightened on the shard, but before he could act, a hand closed over his arm.

"Kael," Alia's voice was calm, yet urgent. "We need to fall back. We can't keep fighting like this.

He whirled to her, his eyes flashing with frustration. "We can't just retreat. Not now. We've come too far."

"I know," she said, her eyes locking with his, "but the city is falling. The walls are coming down. If we stay here, we'll be overrun. We need to regroup, find another way.

Kael's gaze flickered toward the crumbling city gates, the last barrier between them and total annihilation. He could see the enemy pouring through, their dark forms overwhelming the few remaining defenders. It was clear now that Alia was right. They couldn't hold out much longer.

Reluctantly, Kael nodded. "Fall back to the inner keep. We'll make our stand there."

Turning quickly, the group picked up speed, dodging through the battle, narrowly avoiding strikes from the enemy. The city of hope had now seemed to collapse inwards onto itself. Thick billows of smoke wafted into the sky while the air was heavy with the smell of blood and fire. Every corner Kael turned seemed to bring a new wave of enemies, fighting against the tide of some unstoppable force.

As they approached the keep, the last remnants of the defenders of the city could be seen at the gates—a few battered, bloodied soldiers holding it. The faces were grim, the bodies exhausted from the continuous fight that had ensued. But they did not falter, standing firm in their determination to hold the line as long as possible.

Kael approached the gate, his voice hoarse with urgency. "We need to reinforce the walls. Get as many of the injured inside as you can."

The soldier at the gate nodded grimly, barking orders to the others. "We'll hold them as long as we can, but you need to move quickly.

Kael gave a sharp nod, turning to Alia, Rian, and Eryndor, his face hardened with resolve. "It's not over yet. We still have the shard. We can still win this."

Alia wore a look of quiet determination. "And we'll fight alongside you. But we need a plan. The shard alone won't be enough this time."

Kael fisted his hands as he stared out into the chaos. The battlefield was a swirling mess of shadow and violence, a nightmare given form. And the Abyss had come, and they had come in full force.

He wheeled around to the defenders of the keep, exhorting them with one wild cry. "We can win this! But we must fight together. Now is the time to be united, to push back against the darkness. We are not going down without a fight!

The soldiers answered by raising their guns to return fire-a cheer bursting from the mass of them. It was a small moment of unity against amazing odds, and in that instant, Kael felt the surge of hope he so desperately needed.

But hope, he knew, was a fragile thing.

As they prepared for their last stand, a rumble shook the earth beneath their feet. Kael's eyes widened as he looked to the horizon, where a massive, inky black cloud was descending from the sky. The Abyss was not only on the ground; it was in the air as well. A dark, twisted form appeared in the sky above them—a towering figure, its wings spread wide, casting a shadow over the battlefield. The air itself seemed to grow colder in its presence.

That's him," Alia whispered, her voice almost inaudible. "The Lord of the Abyss."

And then the giant form descended to land with a bone-shaking crash at the center of the battlefield. The ground cracked under its weight, and the dark energy pouring from it was palpable as if some kind of suffocating fog was cast down on everything within its environs.

Kael's heart was racing in his chest. He had known the Lord of the Abyss would come. He had felt his presence in the shard, felt the pull of the creature's dark power. This was the final confrontation. And it would not be easy.

"We have to fight him," Kael said, his voice steady despite his fear gnawing at his insides. "We have no choice.

"But the shard..." Rian began, doubt creeping into his voice. "It's not enough to defeat him. It's not enough to defeat this."

Alia stepped forward, her eyes never leaving the Lord of the Abyss. "It's not just the shard. It's us. We must unite all our strength—our will, our purpose. Only together can we defeat him."

Kael nodded, clenching his hand tighter around the shard. "We have no other choice."

Before them stood the Lord of the Abyss, his eyes afire with malignant light. His body was shrouded in a swirl of shadow, and he was towering, with wings trenched wide around him, dark and leathered, as if carved from the very night itself. His face was obscured by a mask of darkness, but Kael felt the coldness emanating from him-icy cold that reached into his soul.

You think you can stop me?" The voice of the Lord of the Abyss boomed, a low, echoing sound that reverberated in Kael's chest. "You are but mortals, nothing more than insects beneath my feet. You cannot hope to defeat the inevitable.

The anger surged through Kael's body, but he clamped down on it. This was not the time for reckless decisions. Turning, he faced Alia and his companions, eyes ablaze. "We have one chance. We must strike together, with everything we have."

The Lord of the Abyss raised one hand, and the ground shook beneath them. Kael could feel the dark energy swirling in upon the creature, coalescing to a single point of pure power. It was as if the very world was being drained of light—of hope.

But Kael wasn't about to let that happen.

He held the shard up, its light flashing brightly in the darkness closing in around him. The power surged inside of it, and for one moment, Kael felt the full weight of its energy. He was aware of the ancient gods, of all those who had gone before him. He was never alone.

With a mighty roar, he hurled the shard toward the Lord of the Abyss, a beam of pure light tearing through the air. The Lord of the Abyss reacted in an instant, his hand rising to block the attack. But the shard's power was beyond anything he had expected. The light clashed against the darkness in a blinding explosion that sent shockwaves through the battlefield.

Kael stumbled backward, blinded by the brilliant intensity of it. When finally the light dissipated, he opened his eyes to find his heart in his throat.

The Lord of the Abyss still stood, yet the air around him had changed. The dark energy from the creature wavered, and for the first time, Kael saw a flicker of doubt dance in the Lord's eyes.

"This is not over," the creature growled, its voice full of anger. But it was too late. The shard had struck a blow, and the balance was tipping.

With one last, combined effort, Kael and his companions charged forward, their weapons raised high, ready to deliver the final blow.

Together, they would finish the darkness. Together, they would conquer the Lord of the Abyss.

The air was thick with the acrid scent of smoke, and the distant howling of wind. The landscape spread before them was nothing less than a graveyard-burning homes, torn banners, and crumbled statues of fallen heroes. What once was the proud city of Sarnoth, a beacon of civilization in a world overtaken by darkness, now lay in ruins, remnants strewn about like the shattered hopes of its people. It had all come to this: a final stand against the dark forces that sought to consume everything they loved.

Kael stood at the edge of the battlefield, scanning the horizon, where the last remnants of the enemy's army-twisted and monstrous-continued their relentless march. The Lord of the Abyss, that towering nightmare, had retreated for now. But Kael could feel the creature's presence like a dark cloud hanging over them-a constant reminder that their fight was far from over.

How much longer can we hold on?" Alia asked, her voice worn with fatigue. Her face was smeared with dirt, her eyes haunted by the toll this battle had taken upon them all. Beside her, Rian clutched his sword, his knuckles white in his firm grip.

We hold until we can hold no longer," Kael replied, his tone grim but resolute. "There is no other choice. Sarnoth must stand, or the world falls."

Alia nodded silently, her gaze slipping to the ruins of the city. There was a hollowness in her eyes, one that spoke of unspoken terrors and the weight of responsibility. They had been through so much, all of them-such loss, such pain. The shard inside Kael was just another reminder of the power and burden it carried with itself. It was the last hope but also a ticking clock, its energy depleting with every use.

Kael clenched his fists. The shard had been their salvation once before, and now its power was waning after everything they had done. Yet, one strike won a battle, as did one act of bravery and one weapon. This was a battle that required everything they would have: every ounce of strength, every ounce of courage, every shred of hope.

We should find a way to get this over with," Rian said, his voice hoarse from shouting over the din of the battle. "There are so many of them, and the Lord of the Abyss."

"He isn't gone," Kael cut in, clenching his eyes shut. "Neither is the darkness. It's just biding its time, gathering its forces. And we'll need to be prepared for what's next.

The words hung heavy in the air, and for a moment, it seemed the world held its breath-the whole city of Sarnoth was waiting for that final blow. But Kael knew the truth: they could wait no longer. If they were to survive, if the world was to have even a semblance of hope to push back the Abyss, they needed to act now.

"We have one last chance," Kael continued, his voice ringing with urgency. "The shard's power is waning, but it still holds the key to victory. We must combine our strengths, use every ounce of energy we have left, and strike at the heart of the Abyss itself."

Alia looked at him, her brow furrowed in thought. "The heart of the Abyss... you mean the Lord of the Abyss?"

"Aye," Kael said. "But not just him. The very source o' the darkness. The rift that lies beyond the veil. It's the source of all this corruption. If we can reach it, if we can destroy it, then we may be able to sever the Abyss's grip on this world."

Rian shifted uncomfortably, his eyes darting to the horizon where the dark clouds were massing. "And how do we reach it? How do we get to the heart of all this?"

"We don't," Kael said softly. "We draw it here."

A moment of silence passed while the implications of Kael's words sank in. Alia opened her mouth to argue, but Kael raised his hand.

"It's the only way. The Lord of the Abyss is too strong for us to face head-on. But if we can draw him to us, if we can channel the power of the shard one final time, we may be able to strike him down."

Alia's expression was one of deep concern. "And the cost? You know the shard's power is draining, and if you push it too far…

"I know," said Kael, his tone subdued. "But we have no choice."

They fell silent, assimilating the plan. The shard's power had taken its toll on Kael already-physically and mentally, emotionally. With every use of its energy, it was depleting his strength even more, and taking him closer to the precipice of exhaustion. Yet, if it were to be a halt to the Lord of the Abyss, a chance, some certain hope to save Sarnoth, then he would have to risk it.

"Then we will do it," Alia said finally, her voice resolute. "We'll help you draw him out."

Kael nodded then, glad of her determination as the two began to ready themselves against what must be the final confrontation.

Hours passed in nervous preparation. The remaining defenders of Sarnoth had retreated into the central keep, where they might make their last stand. They had managed to reinforce the walls as much as possible, but it was evident that their time was near its end. The shadow of the Lord of the Abyss hovered over them, a grim prophecy. The city had no defenses left to talk of now, no more soldiers, and no reinforcements would come. All that remained were Kael, Alia, Rian, and Eryndor, their ragged group bound together by a single purpose.

Kael stood before the shard, now pulsating with an otherworldly glow. He could feel its power humming beneath his skin, its energy alive in the air around them. It was a perilous thing, a weapon forged in the heart of the Abyss itself, and yet it was their only hope. He closed his eyes, reaching out to the shard with his mind, trying to still the erratic pulses of energy within him.

"What do you need us to do?" Alia's voice cut into his thoughts, and he opened his eyes to find her standing beside him, her expression set with determination.

I need you to help me focus," Kael said. "The power of the shard is unstable. If we are to draw the Lord of the Abyss to us, we must direct its energy in a way we've never done before. We'll need all of us-our combined strength-to guide it."

Rian stepped forward, his face set in grim determination. "Let's do it, then.

Kael filled his lungs with a deep breath, gathering strength. In theory, the idea was simple: Entice the Lord of the Abyss to them before letting the shard loose for all it was worth. In practice, it was a little more complicated. They did not know how much longer the shard's power would last; nor if they could get the creature to come at all.

Kael raised his hand, and Alia, Rian, and Eryndor followed suit. In a circle around the shard, each called to the energy inside them. The ground beneath their feet shook as it started to pulse, bright light swirling around them, casting long shadows against the broken walls of Sarnoth.

"Now," Kael muttered under his breath. "We draw him here.

First, there was nothing. Then, louder even than the crack of thunder, a surge of dark energy had burst from the ground itself. The very sky above them seemed to split asunder-a rent torn in the heavens themselves-and from it tumbled a wave of chilling, malevolent energy. The Lord of the Abyss had answered their call.

"Foolish mortals!" The voice of the Lord of the Abyss boomed from above, dark and filled with hate. "You cannot defeat me! I am eternal!"

Yet Kael was prepared. Giving a last, desperate cry, he thrust the shard forward, sending a beam of searing light toward the rift.

The battle for the soul of Sarnoth had begun.

# 9

# The Heart of the Abyss

The earth trembled beneath their feet, as if the world itself was groaning under the weight of the conflict that raged above and below. Kael could feel the pulse of the shard within him, its energy surging through his veins, hot and wild, like an untamed beast. It was as if the very fabric of reality was unraveling around them, as the Lord of the Abyss gathered its power, preparing to strike down everything in its path. The final battle had begun.

Alia, Rian, Eryndor stood behind him, faces pale but set. The shard's light blazed like a tiny sun between them, casting long shadows over the ruin that was Sarnoth. There could be no turning back now. The Lord of the Abyss had been lured into their trap, but it would prove to be more costly than any of them could know.

We can't wait longer," Kael whispered, his voice low but urgent. "The shard won't last much more, and we have to strike now."

Rian nodded grimly, adjusting the grip of his sword. "Let's do it.

Kael's eyes shifted to the rent in the sky, that swirling darkness that seemed to suck in all before it like a churning maelstrom. That was where the Lord of the Abyss waited for them, its gigantic form hovering just beyond the veil and staring down at them with eyes so full of disdain. It was afraid of no one. It had nothing to be afraid of. They were but mortals, fragile and transitory in the face of eternity.

But Kael had three things the Lord did not factor into his victory: hope, resolve, and the shard's power. It was a perilous gamble, yet it was the only one left on the cards.

"Alia," Kael said quietly, turning to the woman beside him. "You and Rian will have to channel the shard's power through me. Focus. This is our only chance."

Alia gave him a sharp nod, her face set with determination. "We're with you, Kael. We'll hold nothing back."

Rian stepped forward, his eyes fixed on the rift in the sky. "This is it, then. We end it here.

With a deep breath, Kael raised his hand toward the rift, feeling the energy of the shard surge through his arm. It was an indescribable feeling-almost like an extension of his own body, a force greater than himself. The shard had always been a source of power, but now, with the Abyss itself bearing down on them, it was both their weapon and their salvation.

The moment Kael raised his hand, the earth around their feet began to shake violently. The air grew thick with an unnatural heat, as if the very atmosphere itself was being drawn into the rift. They could hear, from a distance, the Lord of the Abyss roar in such a terrifying manner that it echoed around the city and shook the last remnants of hope from the defenders' hearts who were still clinging to the city's walls.

"This it is," Kael said low, a murmur to himself. His heart raced in his chest, but he made his body stay steady. The energy of the shard was wholly inside him now, and when he set his will to it, he could feel the energy reach out toward the rift–like a magnet to its match.

The sky above them broke open further, and the form of the Lord of the Abyss began to take shape. Its body was enormous and amorphous, a shifting mass of shadow and flame. Its eyes–two burning orbs of red–settled on Kael, and it seemed to know just what he planned.

You cannot defeat me, mortal," the Lord's voice boomed, deep and raspy, shaking the earth beneath their feet. "I am beyond your grasp. I am eternal. You and your fragile world are nothing before me."

But Kael did not back down. He had heard it all before. It was not fear that filled him, but purpose. Now, he was ready to face it.

Your time is up," Kael said, his voice steady as he channeled the shard's energy into his outstretched hand.

The force of the blast was overwhelming: a wave of white–hot light erupted from Kael, rippling through the air and tearing apart the very fabric of reality as it surged toward the rift. The energy was so thick with intensity that it twisted and warped the sky above as though the stars themselves were being eaten by the shard.

For a single moment, it seemed as though the world froze.

Then, with a deafening roar, the Lord of the Abyss struck.

The light of the shard versus the dark and sinister forces of the Lord–the collision was cataclysmic. A shockwave rippled outwards, shaking the city to its foundations. Buildings crumbled, the ground tore its face asunder, and the air seemed to explode in fire as the two opposing forces clashed.

Kael felt himself being forced backward; the sheer force of this explosion was on the verge of tearing him asunder. The shard pulsed violently within him, its power growing with every second that passed, yet even its intensive energy was not enough to stop the full force of the Lord's power. It was like the darkness was spilling from this rent in waves, scratching at Kael, Alia, Rian, and Eryndor, attempting to take them down into the depths of despair.

"We cannot hold on much longer!" Alia shouted, her voice strained in the struggle to maintain focus. "Kael, you have to—"

"I know!" Kael yelled back, his voice trembling with the effort of sustaining control. "We have to force it back!"

With a final, desperate scream, Kael put all his last bits of energy into the shard, his body shaking under the strain. The shard's light exploded once more, brighter than the sun could ever be, filling the sky with blinding brilliance.

And then, suddenly, there was silence.

There was complete silence, as if time itself had suddenly come to a halt. The rent in the sky slowly began to heal, the churning darkness receding as the light from the shard drove it back.

Kael fell to his knees, his body sapping to an unbelievable extreme. The energy in the shard was almost drained; the light trembled weakly in his hand. He'd given everything he had, and still, the world hung in the balance.

Alia knelt beside him, her hand on his shoulder, her eyes wide with concern. "Kael, we did it... didn't we?

Rian stood a few feet away, his sword still drawn, watching the sky intently. "I don't know. It's over... isn't it?"

The rift was closing, but a feeling of foreboding still lingered. Kael's breath was ragged, his vision blurred, but he knew that the battle was far from over. The Lord of the Abyss had been forced back, but it was not truly gone. There was still the matter of the heart of the Abyss, the source of the darkness that had plagued their world.

We haven't won yet," Kael muttered under his breath. "The heart of the Abyss is still out there. And as long as it exists, the darkness will return."

Alia's eyes widened as realization dawned on her. "What do you mean? We drew it out. We struck it down. The rift is closing. The Lord of the Abyss... it's over.

Kael weakly shook his head. "The Lord of the Abyss was just a servant. The true heart of the darkness is beyond that rift, in the very heart of the void. And as long as it exists, it's going to keep coming back."

Rian ground his teeth. "Then what do we do now?

Kael struggled to his feet, his body protesting every movement. "We have to destroy the heart, once and for all. If we don't..."

His voice trailed off, failing him as he fought to remain conscious. The last remnants of the shard's power were slipping away, and he knew he had only moments before he collapsed.

"We must go after it," Kael finished, his voice a bare rasp. "Before it regains its strength."

The three of them exchanged wordless glances, the weight of what still lay ahead settling heavy in their stomachs. There was no turning back now. The heart of the Abyss was their last enemy, and they would either face it and destroy it, or they would die in trying.

With a final glance at the now-closing rift, they headed into their last destination: the heart of the Abyss, prepared once again to face the darkness.

The world around them was changing.

The trembling of the earth beneath his boots could be felt by Kael, as he, Alia, Rian, and Eryndor pressed onward, their journey carrying them ever closer to the heart of the Abyss. The air itself seemed to hum with the dark energy emanating from the rift they had just sealed. Even now, with the rift itself closing and the darkness being thrown back, there was an undeniable weight pressing down upon them. The heart of the Abyss was not so easily defeated.

The shard that once pulsed with power within Kael had now barely a flicker, its light waning with each step. He felt it, how the shard's energy had been drawn to its core. The energy they had spent to push back the Lord of the Abyss came with a great cost; what was now left within Kael was just mere remnants, a mere whisper in the storm.

Still, there was no choice but to move forward.

"There's no turning back," Kael said quietly, his voice steady but weary. "We have to destroy it, no matter the cost."

Alia nodded, her eyes shining with determination. Though exhaustion weighed heavy on their shoulders, her will did not bend. She saw what the battle had taken from her comrades, and knew she could not afford to do less than press on now. Finish this, or they would have fought for nothing.

The practical Rian looked to the horizon. The path before them was dark, the once-bright city of Sarnoth now a shadow of its former glory. Broken buildings and shattered streets lined their way, remnants of the devastation that the Lord of the Abyss had wrought before it was forced back. But as Kael had said, this was far from over. The heart of the Abyss-to-come now lay before him, its malignant influence stretching like a suffocating cloud across the land.

Eryndor, the elven sorcerer, remained speechless as always, gazing at the horizon. His years had taught him to know the lurking peril in this air, the signs of an oncoming storm. He could sense there was something ancient and terrible standing just beyond the veil. It was close, so close, and it had been waiting for them. The final confrontation was here.

They pressed on, the tension thickening with each step. As they neared the heart of the Abyss, the ground beneath their feet began to crack-fissures splitting open in the earth as if the very fabric of their world was unraveling. The air thickened into a noisome, heavy energy that threatened suffocation. It was a feeling in the chest, like a weight pushing against his lungs, and yet he pushed ahead. They were too close now.

"The heart is near," Eryndor muttered, as the voice was almost snatched away by a sudden, howling wind that had sprung up. "I can feel its pulse. It's... waiting."

Kael could hear the sorcerer's words, but they felt distant. Everything was becoming distant. The exhaustion in his limbs was unbearable, and yet he couldn't stop. He couldn't afford to stop.

"I'm not going to let it win," Kael whispered, more to himself than to his companions.

Alia placed a reassuring hand on his shoulder, her voice steady. "We're with you, Kael. All the way."

Soon after, they reached the heart of the Abyss: a twisted, malformed mass of shadow and energy, floating just above the ground in a sea of swirling darkness. The air around it was alive with the pulse of unholy power, the very essence of corruption which had spread across their world. The Heart of the Abyss was not just any mere physical form, but the condensation of that darkness from which all this evil emanated.

The heart seemed to beat with a more concentrated wickedness as Kael and his companions drew near. It tested every step they took with a power that repelled them. In Kael's hand, the shard's light flared, its energy sputtering like a candle in the wind.

The heart, a churning, massive cloud of darkness and radiating light, seemed to acknowledge their presence. The ground started to shake beneath their feet as the heart began to swell further and further with each passing second.

Kael's heart began to race. There was no turning back now.

"We have to destroy it," Kael said, his voice tight with the effort of keeping himself steady. "We need to use the shard's last bit of power."

Alia stepped forward, her eyes narrowed with concentration. "We're ready, Kael. Do it."

Kael took a deep breath and raised the shard toward the heart. What little energy still resided within the shard flared to life once more; the last remnants of its power answered his call. The shard lit up, its light illuminating the surrounding darkness, pushing the shadows away for a moment before they closed in again.

The heart pulsed in response, sending waves of dark energy that hit Kael hard like a tidal wave. Stumbling backward, he felt his body weaken from the attack. The darkness seemed to wrap itself around him, pulling him down, but he refused to go. He squeezed the shard harder and suddenly shouted loudly as he finally pushed the last energy from it, channeling toward the heart of the Abyss all the power he could appeal to.

The world exploded.

A blinding flash of light filled the air as the shard's energy surged forward, striking the heart of the Abyss with the force of a thousand storms. The shockwave sent Kael and his companions sprawling, throwing them backward as the ground around them cracked open. The heart shuddered, its surface rippling and warping under the impact of the light.

For a moment, everything was silent. The world seemed to hang in the balance, suspended between life and death.

Then, the heart began to scream.

The sound was deafening–a ghastly, inhuman wail that tore at the very fabric of reality. The ground beneath them burst open, sending great slabs of earth hurling into the air. The sky itself seemed to writhe, twisting and buckling beneath the force of the heart's agony. Kael's heart raced in his chest as he struggled to remain conscious, his body wracked with pain from the explosion of energy.

The shard in his hand flickered weakly, its light growing dimmer with each second that passed. Kael knew it could not last much longer. He was running on empty. They all were.

"It's not enough!" Alia cried out in a desperate voice. "We need more power!"

Kael gritted his teeth. "There is no more power. We have to finish this now."

Kael made himself stand, using the last of his strength. He felt the darkness encroaching again, the heart of the Abyss tugging everything toward it. But he refused to give in. Not now. Not after all they had endured.

"Alia, Rian, Eryndor," Kael said in a hoarse voice, but with all resolution. "We finish this together."

The three nodded, their eyes flint-like with resolve. They knew this was it. If they failed here, the world would slide into eternal darkness. They were the last line of defense, and they would not fail.

Kael raised his hand once more, channeling the last of his strength into the shard. Energy crackled through the air as he called upon the shard's power, forcing it to its limits. The shard responded with a surge of light, brighter than before, and this time, the heart of the Abyss did not scream. It writhed in agony, yet the heart itself seemed to begin to break apart under the force of their combined efforts.

The heart of the Abyss exploded in one deafening roar.

A wave of light and shadow cascaded outwards, engulfing everything in its path. The blast was so strong that Kael could feel his very soul being pulled apart, as if the fabric of reality was being torn at the seams. The world around them seemed to bend and twist, and for a moment, Kael thought they might all be lost.

Then, in an instant, it was silent.

When Kael opened his eyes, the world had changed. The heart of the Abyss was gone, reduced to nothing more than a distant memory. The darkness that had plagued their world for so long had finally been vanquished.

They had won.

But the victory came at a cost.

Kael's gaze circled around his companions, worn from what their fight had taken. Alia, Rian, and Eryndor were all battered and bruised, the color of their faces pale with exhaustion. They had all given everything, and in that moment, Kael knew they had saved the world.

But it was clear that this was not the end. The journey had taken its toll on them all, and the world would need to rebuild. The Abyss had been defeated, but the scars would remain.

"We did it," Kael said, his voice filled with a mixture of relief and sorrow. "But we've lost so much."

Alia placed a hand on his shoulder, her eyes filled with understanding. "We've lost a lot, Kael. But we've also gained something. Hope. A future. We've saved this world."

And with that, they stood together, looking out over the land they had fought to protect, knowing that their battle was over—but their journey had only just begun.

# 10

# Light at the Break of Dawn

The light of the rising sun broke through the remnants of the dark clouds that had once shrouded the land in perpetual gloom. It was a moment of quiet, a moment of reckoning. The world was healing, but the scars of their battle remained. In the distance, the ruined city of Sarnoth stood silent, a haunting reminder of the price they had paid for victory. But beyond the wreckage, the earth was slowly coming alive again, the first tendrils of green sprouting from the blackened soil, the promise of renewal after the destruction.

Kael stood at the edge of the ruined battlefield, his eyes fixed on the horizon. His body screamed with the weight of everything they had endured, but the exhaustion was different now. It was the exhaustion of a battle well-fought—a long, treacherous journey that had reached its conclusion. And yet, in the stillness that followed, there was a sense of uncertainty—a question that loomed in his mind: what now?

He had done it. The Abyss was defeated, and the heart of darkness destroyed. The rift had been sealed, and the power that had once threatened to consume their world had been vanquished. But the victory was bittersweet. Kael had lost so much along the way—his comrades had paid dearly, and the world itself would never be the same. The land was broken, the cities shattered, and lives lost. The cost of their salvation had come at a price much higher than any of them had ever thought it would.

"Kael," Alia's voice cut into his thoughts, and he turned to see her walking towards him. Her face was tired, her eyes haunted by the same sense of loss that weighed heavily on his own heart. And yet, there was something else there too, a flicker of hope, a light that could not be extinguished.

"We did it," she whispered, but her voice was firm. "We saved the world. We did what we came here to do."

Kael nodded, though the words tasted empty in his mouth. "We saved it. but at what cost? So much has been lost. The world is shattered."

Alia fell into step beside him, her gaze tracing the horizon where the sun had begun to rise. "Yes, the world is broken," she agreed. "But it's not beyond repair. We gave it a chance. And that's more than anybody else could have done."

Kael shot a glance at her, marking resolution in her expression. "But can it really heal? Can we rebuild what we've lost?"

"We have to," Alia replied. "We don't have a choice. The future is ours now. It's in our hands."

As she spoke, Kael noticed Rian and Eryndor approaching. The elven sorcerer's face was solemn, his expression unreadable, but Rian's was filled with the same weariness they all carried. Their eyes met, and for a moment, the weight of everything that had happened hung between them, unsaid.

"We've lost so much," Rian said quietly, his voice low. "But we've also gained so much. The people of Sarnoth, of our world—they have a chance to rebuild. To rise from the ashes, just as we have."

Kael turned his gaze back to the ruined city. He could almost see the memories of the battles they had fought, the streets that had been ravaged, the lives lost in the fight against the darkness. But Rian was right. There was hope. It wasn't much, but it was enough to keep going.

"We can rebuild," Eryndor said, quiet wisdom laced within his voice. "It would take some time, though. We have to start it now, while the land is still in a process of healing. People must come united, as we can regain only through unity what has been lost."

The weight of their words settled upon Kael's shoulders. He had been so bent on defeating the heart of the Abyss, on saving the world from its corruption, that he hadn't given as much thought to afterward-the long road of recovery ahead. It wasn't enough that the war should end. Rebuilding needed to start now, and it would be up to them-the survivors-to lead the way.

"We have work to do," Kael said finally, and there was steel in his tone now. "This is just the start. The land will heal, but it will have to be guided. The people will need leaders, and we're the ones who'll have to lead them."

Alia nodded. "Together."

The four of them stood in silence, observing the sun rise higher in the sky and cast its warm, golden glow over the ruins of Sarnoth. It was a sign of new beginnings, a sign that even through the blackest of times, light could still break through. Standing thus, they knew this was their moment-no longer mere survivors of the war, but architects of the time to come.

Kael took a deep breath, letting the sun's warmth wash over him. There was much to do, but for the first time in a long while, he felt a flicker of hope. They had defeated the darkness, but now it was time to rebuild, not just the world, but the very spirit of those that had fought for it.

The first steps were always the hardest, but Kael knew they would take them together. It had been a long journey, the price steep, but well worth the reward: a world that had been saved from the brink of destruction. And now it was their duty to see that it remained safe, that it prospered, and that the foul mistakes of their past were never revisited.

With every step that Kael, Alia, Rian, and Eryndor took towards the heart of the ruined city, survivors began to join their ranks. Everyone from across the kingdom, even from the lowliest villages, emerged in the aftermath of the battle. The rubble of Sarnoth began to rise again, teeming with life as people went to work rebuilding what had been taken away, brick by brick and stone by stone.

Kael couldn't help the feeling of awe as he looked around. The world was broken, yes, but not the people in it. They were steadfast, strong, and resilient to rise from the ashes. He had seen the darkness once gripping them, the hopelessness which had almost torn them asunder. Now, though-in the aftermath of their victory-Kael saw another thing: a spark, a flicker of light that would carry them onward.

The path would be a long one, with many challenges. There were wounds that would not heal in a single day, and there was still the reality of dangers lurking in the darkness. But Kael knew, as long as they stood together, they could face whatever came next. The world was theirs to rebuild, and they would do it with the same courage and determination that had carried them through the darkest days of the Abyss.

"We've made it this far," Kael said, his voice steady and resolute. "We'll make it the rest of the way."

Alia smiled at him, her eyes filled with that same unwavering resolve. "To-gether."

And together, they would face the future.

Days went by, and rebuilding continued. Survivors of Sarnoth and other people from all over the land worked day and night to restore their homes and lives. The city, once ruined, began to take shape again; its streets were alive with the sound of building, with life coming back into the world. The land, too, began healing, as if in recognition of the endeavors of those that saved it.

At the forefront of this endeavor stood Kael, Alia, Rian, and Eryndor-those who had guided the people into reclaiming their world. The lessons of yesteryear-the mistakes and sacrifices-would not be forgotten but would live on to be passed down and shared with the next generation to make sure the terrors of the Abyss would never be repeated.

It was slow, but it was progress.

And Kael, looking out over the land he had fought to save, knew that while the scars of the past would still be there, the future now lay theirs to shape.

The final chapter in their journey had been written, yet the story was far from at an end.

The dawn of new beginnings had come.

The sun had risen high in the sky, casting its warm, golden glow across the world. It had been just another day, yet somehow different. The air felt lighter, the earth seemed to breathe easier, and for the first time in a long time, Kael felt the weight of the past lifting from his shoulders. The battle had been fought, the enemy defeated, and now the long road of rebuilding was well underway.

He stood at the edge of the newly reconstructed city of Sarnoth, looking out over the horizon to where the first signs of spring were beginning to take root. Lands that once had lain barren, ravaged by the forces of the Abyss, now bore the tender green shoots of renewal. The world, broken and scarred, was healing. But it had been a healing process that was not exactly instant; rather, it was slow and sure, a testimony to the resilience of people who had fought to preserve it.

Kael's mind wandered back to the beginning of this journey, to the days when the darkness had seemed insurmountable. It was a battle that tested their strength, will, and even hearts. He had lost so much on the way through friends, comrades, and mentors. But he had gained so much more than he could have ever imagined-the bonds they had formed, the alliances they had forged, and the hope they had spurred in the people's hearts-all that was worth the sacrifice.

But it wasn't just the victory over the Abyss that made this moment so important. It was the understanding that they weren't done; the world may have been saved from the darkness, but the task of guiding it into the light had just begun.

As Kael stood in silent reflection, he heard the sound of footsteps approaching from behind. He turned to see Alia walking toward him, her steps steady and purposeful. She had become a leader in her own right, a symbol of hope for the people who had watched her grow from a reluctant warrior to a fierce protector. There was a quiet strength in her eyes, a resilience that mirrored his own.

"It's hard to believe it's really over," she said softly, her voice carrying the weight of their shared experiences. "After everything we've been through, the world is finally starting to heal."

Kael nodded, a bittersweet smile tugging at the corners of his lips. "It is. But the healing is only just beginning. We've done our part, but now it's up to the people. It's up to all of us to rebuild what was lost."

Alia came to stand beside him at the edge of the city, her gaze tracing the course of the river as it snaked its way through the valley below. "You don't think they will remember what happened? The price paid in order to save them?"

"I hope so," Kael said quietly. "I hope they remember the sacrifices-the ones who fought and fell to make this world a better place. The fallen... they deserve to be remembered."

"They will be," Alia asserted, her tone firm. "Their names will be carried forward, their stories told to the next generation. We can't afford to forget."

In a solemn gathering, the survivors of the battle who had come to pay their respects to the fallen heroes trooped along the hill towards them; they stood side by side. They were carrying wreaths of flowers and banners draped with the symbols of their fallen comrades. Present among them was Rian, who had been a central column in support throughout the journey. The sound of his presence was calming, a steady anchor within the storm.

Kael watched as the people congregated in the center of the hill, a place that once saw fierce fighting and was now a place for peace and contemplation. The names of the fallen were called one by one, their stories shared, their sacrifice honored. With each name came a moment of silence, a collective acknowledgment of the weight of their loss.

And the names of the dead termed out loud, one by one, while Kael's heart was wrung with an intolerable ache. The faces swam before his eyes: friends and comrades, their laughter, their bravery, their unyielding resolution. He knew them all, as only a man who has fought beside them in battle can know them. They were his kin, not of blood, but of common purpose. And they were gone.

He closed his eyes a moment, letting the memories wash over him. He could still hear their voices, still feel the presence of those who had fought by his side. They would never truly be gone: their legacy living on in the stories they had shared, the lessons they had taught, and the world they had helped save.

When Kael opened his eyes again, he found that he was not alone. Alia, Rian, and Eryndor stood beside him, their faces somber but set. Together, they had faced the darkness, and together they would make certain it never returned.

Rian spoke first, ever the quiet philosopher. "The people will look to us for guidance, Kael. But we cannot do this alone. We must build alliances, forge new relationships with the neighboring kingdoms. The threat of darkness may be gone, but there are still challenges ahead. We must remain vigilant.

Kael nodded in agreement. "I know. The war is over, but the real work is just beginning. We need to make sure that the peace we fought for will last."

Eryndor, the elven sorcerer, laid a hand on Kael's shoulder. "There will always be challenges. But we've proven that we can face them. Together.

And in the flash of a quiet determination, Alia said, "We've lost so much, but we have gained something far greater: the people's trust. They believe in us. And that is the foundation upon which we will build the future.

As the service went on, a peace had come upon Kael. These people had gathered not simply to morn their fallen comrades but to celebrate the new dawn that had come. That was the moment of communal self-reflection, a homage to times past, with a step toward the future.

Later that evening, when the ceremony was finally over and the people had returned to their homes, Kael stood alone at the heart of the city and let his gaze slide over the horizon. A spattering of stars was starting to flash across the sky, a reminder that though night would always fall, so too would the dawn.

In the distance, the sounds of rebuilding echoed down the streets. The people were working: repairing homes, tending to crops, and rebuilding their lives. The world was slowly, bit by bit, healing. The darkness had been driven back, but the work of healing was far from over.

Kael knew the legacy of those fallen lived on in the work ahead; that their sacrifice had not been in vain, and it had paved a certain path for a better future-such that the mistakes of the past would not be repeated, such that darkness would never again hold sway over the world.

The wind whispered through the trees, carrying with it the promise of new beginnings. He felt a great sense of gratitude, not just for the world they had saved but for those people who fought alongside him. The fallen were gone, but their legacy would live on in the hearts of the people who had survived. Their stories would be passed down, their names would be remembered, and the lessons they had taught would shape the world for generations to come.

As Kael turned to leave, a final thought remained in his mind: this was not the end, it was but a beginning. Long and uncertain would be the road ahead, but so long as they stood together, Kael knew that whatever challenges lay ahead they would face.

The world had been saved, but now it was time to rebuild. And in the rebuilding, Kael knew that the legacy of the ones fallen would live on. It would shape the future, guide the forthcoming generations, and see to it that the light would always shine, come whatever night.

Together they would author a new chapter in their saga. And in so doing, they would remember the fallen and forge a future worthy of their sacrifice.

And with that, a legacy of the fallen well and truly lived on.

# About the Author

About the Author

**Jackson Grisham** is a storyteller at heart, weaving tales of courage, adventure, and the eternal struggle between light and darkness. A lifelong lover of epic fantasy and adventure, Jackson draws inspiration from timeless classics and modern challenges alike, creating narratives that resonate with readers of all ages.

When not lost in the worlds of his own making, Jackson can often be found exploring the great outdoors, indulging in his passion for travel, or discovering new books to devour. With a deep appreciation for mythology, history, and the power of the human spirit, Jackson's works reflect his belief in the resilience of hope and the beauty of unity.

**Elarion's Legacy** marks another step in his journey as a writer—a saga that seeks to inspire, challenge, and remind us all of the heroes we carry within.

Jackson lives with his family and a loyal canine companion, who often serves as his sounding board for new ideas. He invites readers to join him on his adventures and connect through his website or social media.